THE FOOTLIGHTS MURDER

Esther & Jack Enright Mystery
Book Twelve

David Field

SAPERE
BOOKS

THE
FOOTLIGHTS
MURDER

Published by Sapere Books.

24 Trafalgar Road, Ilkley, LS29 8HH

saperebooks.com

ISBN: 978-0-85495-819-1

CHAPTER ONE

London, 1905

It was the final night of their successful run of *Julius Caesar*, and the Holborn Players were performing to a capacity crowd on the upper floor of their rented premises in Endell Street. It was yet another commendably visualised show, produced under the guidance of the troupe's director, Lucy Masefield, who was standing proudly in the wings with a broad smile on her face. They had reached Act 3, Scene 1, and so far the amateur production had, like the previous four, gone without a positional hitch or a missed cue.

Caesar had ignored both the earlier warnings of the soothsayer and the attempt by Artemidorus to warn him of the evil intentions of the conspirators, and was holding forth in the Capitol, arrogantly rejecting the petition of a man seeking to have his brother returned from exile. The conspirators gathered round the emperor in a huddled group, seemingly intent on supporting the petitioner, then in a series of flashes caught perfectly by the tracker spotlight, the knives were out, hacking into the flesh beneath the toga.

Lead actor Valentine Primrose appeared to have forgotten his most famous line — *"Et tu, Brute? Then fall, Caesar"* — and Lucy looked urgently down to the front row of the audience, hoping that the prompter could rescue the moment. Then her attention was drawn urgently back to the stage when she heard a scream from Leopold Carter, in his role as Cassius. She became aware of the remainder of the group backing away in silent horror, transfixed by the sight of real blood oozing out from under the rapidly reddening toga of the now prone man they were supposed to be only pretending to assassinate.

She shouted for the curtains to be closed, then stepped in front of them to assure the audience that they were experiencing a temporary technical problem, and that the play would resume with only the briefest delay. Some of them were already donning their hats and coats as she pushed back through the heavy drapes and hurried over to the bleeding man. Several pairs of Roman sandals had been soiled by the spray.

'Do you think he's *really* dead?' Arthur Dennistoun asked.

'We won't know unless we call a doctor — a *real* one, that is, not a fancy West End one like Henry,' said Simon Abelman. 'Lucy, could you find out if there's one in the audience?'

There were several, but it was a Dr Wilberforce Pearce, a police surgeon enjoying a rare evening off, who pushed his way through the horrified throng. He leaned over the still form of the lead actor and confirmed, 'Life extinct, I'm afraid. Someone call the police without delay, and everyone remain where they are.'

'It must have been an accident,' suggested a traumatised Leopold Carter, until five minutes ago a leading conspirator in the play. 'I never *did* trust those bloody stage props. Lucy, did you check them before we went on?'

'Of *course* I did!' Lucy insisted. 'I checked them *every* night, just before you all collected them from the table in the dressing room. I have no idea what went wrong.'

They were still on stage, some of them seated because their legs had become understandably wobbly, when ten minutes later two uniformed policemen appeared. They began taking names and addresses ahead of the arrival of Inspector Buxton and Sergeant Leonard from nearby Grays Inn Road Police

Station, summoned by a third constable who had run back there without pausing when he saw what they were dealing with.

The inspector held his badge high in the air as he announced his rank. 'I'm from the Metropolitan Police, E Division. Who's in charge here?'

'I suppose I am,' said Lucy shakily. 'Lucy Masefield, Producer and Director.'

'And who was responsible for these knives being issued to the actors?'

'That was me as well. I was doubling as the stage manager — we're only an amateur group, you see.'

'I'll be collecting them all, although the one that did the damage is obviously still in the corpse,' the inspector observed bluntly.

Leopold whimpered in response, while Simon clicked his teeth disapprovingly.

'I think it was *my* knife,' Leopold admitted in a quavering voice. 'It felt different from rehearsals, when it just went "click". This time I felt it go into soft flesh, and the blood spurted all over my toga, as you can see. Can I take it off, please? Otherwise I fear I'm going to be sick.'

'We'll need *all* your clothing in due course,' Inspector Buxton told them, 'so you may as well all get changed into your usual clothes, and hand your costumes to one of my constables. I'll also need you back out here on stage once you've changed, so that we can make a record of who was standing where when this tragic event occurred. We'll need full statements from you all in due course. Who was the deceased, Miss?' he asked Lucy as the actors slipped back to their dressing room.

'Mrs,' Lucy insisted. 'I'm Mrs Lucy Masefield. My husband has an architectural practice in Southampton Place, and we live in the rooms above it.'

'That doesn't tell me who the deceased was.'

'Sorry, that was Valentine Primrose, one of our most valued actors, in the role of Julius Caesar. He lives — sorry, *lived* — in nearby Mayfair somewhere, but I'd need to look in our records for his precise address.'

'Was he married, or is there some other next of kin we should inform?'

'A bachelor, so far as I'm aware. Reputed to be "the other way inclined", if you follow me, so most probably no children, either.'

'Very well, I'll get someone to look into that. Now, it looks as if your actors are returning, and we can restage what actually happened.'

'I should have thought it was obvious what happened,' Lucy replied tersely. 'The real questions are surely "why" and "who planned it", are they not?'

'That's my business,' Buxton replied coldly. 'Now, could you recreate the scene at the time of death, please?'

The actors, now dressed in the clothes they had been wearing when they arrived for that evening's performance, regathered in a traumatised group, Leopold almost in tears. 'The inspector wants you to take up your positions at the moment of the assassination,' Lucy told them, then turned to Buxton. 'There'll be one missing, of course,' she reminded him. 'Would you like me to stand where the actor playing Caesar was standing?'

'No, I'll need you to direct the re-enactment, and ensure that it's exactly the same as it was,' Buxton replied. 'I'll also need to observe precisely what happens, so we'll find a use for one of mine, shall we? Constable Reilly!' he called out. 'Here's your chance to perform on the stage — over here, please.'

The young constable did as he was told, and stood, as directed by Lucy, as close as possible to the position occupied by the deceased immediately before his death. 'Very well,' said Buxton, 'play it as it was scripted — but without knives this time, obviously.'

The actors grouped around the constable, and Lucy gave them the cue line, which was 'Doth not Brutus bootless kneel?' The actors then swarmed in, with Brutus rising from his knees to confront the uniformed constable directly, joined immediately by Cassius in the person of Leopold, from the side.

Casca, Cinna and Decius did their best to lean over the constable's shoulder, and it was Arthur, as Casca, who objected, 'This police constable's much taller than poor old Val was, so it can't be exactly reproduced.'

'It doesn't *need* to be, does it?' Leopold wailed. 'It was *my* knife, and I don't think I'll ever be able to forget that feeling when it jammed.' He broke into racking sobs and crumpled onto the boards, to be consoled by Ernest Graves with a hand on his shoulder.

'Very well,' Buxton conceded, 'I think we can dispense with the re-enactment. But did any of the rest of you feel what this gentleman did? The knife actually entering the flesh, that is?'

Leopold gave another wail and began shaking violently.

'Is the doctor still here?' Buxton asked Lucy. 'If so, perhaps he can give something to this poor chap, to calm him down for long enough for someone to get an intelligible statement out of him.'

'The man's in shock, for God's sake,' Simon protested. 'Aren't you supposed to make allowances for a suspect's emotional state when you interview him?'

'I'm not yet interviewing him,' Buxton said, bristling, 'and he's not yet a suspect. But what do *you* know about police procedures? Encountered them in the past, have you?'

'I'm a barrister at law,' Simon replied haughtily, 'and I'm just saying that this man should not be interviewed while he's in such an emotionally vulnerable state.'

'He won't be,' Buxton told him testily. 'Once we've got his full name and address, he can go home, as can the rest of you once you've supplied the same information. Right now, I'm more interested in the knives — where they were kept, who was guarding them until they were needed, how they were designed so as not to inflict injuries on the actors, and how one of them was clearly substituted.'

'There was no substitution,' Lucy replied in a shaking voice, 'assuming that the one with the blood on it — the one that your constable put into a bag just then — was the one that killed Valentine Primrose, the actor playing Caesar. I haven't seen it close up again since — well, since the tragic accident — but from a distance it looked like one of ours. My first instinct is that the retracting mechanism must have failed for some horrible reason or other.'

'So tell me about this "retracting mechanism", as you call it,' Buxton replied. 'Precisely what steps did you take to ensure that all the knives were safe to use?'

'They were kept on a table in the main dressing room,' Lucy explained. 'I can take you there if you wish, and if you let me use one of the other knives for a brief moment, I can show you what was supposed to happen. But before that, may my distraught friends here go home?'

'Very well,' Buxton agreed, 'once we've got all their personal details, so that we can contact them again and take full statements later.'

After the actors had left, Lucy took Buxton backstage into the large dressing room, where the actors usually assembled after donning their costumes in what amounted to changing cubicles down one side. Lucy pointed to a large table in the centre, on which sat two large flagons of lemon juice, a dozen or so glass tumblers, and two plates of sandwiches that had been intended for the cast and stage crew after the performance.

'This table would have been all but empty before the performance began, and indeed until halfway through it,' she explained. 'My assistant stage manager, Alice Bennett, prepared the refreshments, and would have brought them in just after the start of the third act, when the last of the props had been taken onstage by the actors, so that the table would have been empty again by then. Feel free to help yourself, since obviously the actors won't be requiring them now. It would be a shame to let them go to waste.'

'Let's concentrate on the knives, shall we?' Buxton replied tersely. 'First of all, how many were there?'

'Let me see now…' Lucy counted on her fingers. 'Eight altogether. There was one each for Brutus, Cassius, Casca, Cinna and Decius — they were the "conspirators" in the play who were planning on killing Caesar, so that's five accounted for. We have several more in the store cupboard, if you'd like me to demonstrate how they work.'

Buxton nodded his agreement, so Lucy opened a cupboard on one of the walls and extracted what looked like a vicious dagger. 'These don't come cheaply,' she told Buxton, 'but we managed to get eight from a professional theatre in Drury Lane that closed down some months ago. It pays to be well connected in the theatrical world, and I once worked for them as a voluntary assistant stage manager when they fell on hard times, prior to their final financial collapse.'

'Just show me how they work,' Buxton said sternly, unimpressed by the knives' origins.

Lucy held one out in front of her face, tested it briefly, then with a dramatic flourish brought the knife down onto her left palm. There was an audible clicking sound, and the hilt appeared to bury itself in her hand, with no spurt of blood and no expression of pain on her face.

'As you can see, it's retractable,' she told Buxton. 'Actors have been using these commonplace props for years, and I've never heard of any accidents. There's a risk that the retracting mechanism will stick due to dampness or rust, so every evening, sometime before the start of the third act, which opens with the assassination scene, I'd check every one of them to ensure that they were operating freely. An actor hit by one might end up with a bruise, but nothing worse.'

'And you checked them this evening in accordance with this normal practice?'

'I did indeed. I had plenty of time, because there was a ten-minute interlude between the second and third acts.'

'During which time the actors would have been offstage, and in here?'

'Either in here, or using one of the lavatories, or perhaps standing at the stage door, having a smoke. The terms of our lease prohibit smoking in this building, to minimise the fire risk.'

'When you checked the knives this evening, who was in here with you, if anyone?'

'Let me see now…' Lucy closed her eyes in order to improve her memory. 'There was Val — Valentine Primrose, the man who died. He was always nervous before going on stage, and a bit of an old woman about remembering his lines, so he was over there behind me somewhere.' She indicated with a backward wave of her hand. 'I'm pretty sure Leo — Leopold Carter — was in here as well, over there.' She gestured forward. 'He took his acting seriously, and was pacing nervously up and down — and getting on my nerves, to be honest. I checked the knives, then went out to ensure that the scenery was in place for the Capitol scene.'

'Leaving the deceased and this man "Carter" in here alone?'

'Probably, because I don't remember anyone else being in here when I went out. They would all have had to come through here to access the stage, of course, and each would have picked up a knife as they did so.'

'So anyone could have interfered with one of those knives, even the man who wielded it, then made such a big fuss when his turned out to be the fatal blow? Wasn't that Carter, the man who was left in here alone with the deceased?'

Lucy couldn't help laughing. 'Forgive me, but the thought of dear old Leo being a murderer is almost farcical. He's a sweet little pussycat, and so gentle that he regularly gets ragged about it by the others in the company. He was also very fond of Val. Are you seriously suggesting that he could have fiddled with the knife under the very nose of the man who he was intent on murdering? And in any case, we don't know that the knife *was* interfered with, do we? My guess is that the mechanism became jammed.'

'Didn't you just tell me that you'd examined them carefully in order to eliminate that possibility?'

'Yes, and I did, I can assure you. But nothing will stop me thinking that Val's death was somehow all my fault. That despite what I thought was a careful check, I missed something. These actions can become *too* routine, of course, meaning that perhaps we're not as fastidious as we ought to be in performing them.'

'Well, the knife's been sent off for testing, so we'll know soon enough,' Buxton told her. 'Now, is there anyone else here that I need to speak to?'

'I don't think so,' Lucy replied. 'There was a lighting person, who would have been in the gallery up behind the back row of the audience, and a stagehand operating the curtains and other stage equipment, but I told them they could go home after the actors left. I hope that was in order.'

'Probably not, but give me their names and addresses and we'll follow it up. Is there anyone else you sent home without authorisation from me?'

'There was Sophia Grundy, the prompter,' Lucy replied, somewhat shamefaced. 'She was sitting in the front row of the audience, and it was her job to give an actor their next line if they forgot.'

'So she would have seen everything?'

'Of course, but no more than we demonstrated to you when we did that re-enactment. And haven't we established how it happened? A knife that didn't retract, in the hand of a devastated Leo Carter?'

'*We* haven't decided anything, Mrs Masefield. It's my job to decide what happened, and who was responsible. And I'll thank you not to make any more, no doubt well-meaning, efforts to conduct my enquiry for me. Now, let's see if this Sophia Grundy's still available to speak to me, shall we?'

CHAPTER TWO

Percy Enright smiled lovingly as thirteen-year-old Annabelle Pickering caught hold of the toy boat she'd been sailing on the lake in Victoria Park, Hackney. She lifted it out of the water, shook the excess from its keel and walked back up the grassy bank to where 'Uncle Percy' was waiting for her, seated on a bench. He wasn't her real uncle, and he most certainly wasn't her father, but she already felt, to him, like his granddaughter. For a man in his late sixties who'd never had children, she was like a gift from God.

Annabelle had come into the Enright family when Esther Enright, Percy's nephew Jack's wife, who was her schoolteacher, had taken her in following a series of tragic events that had rendered her an orphan. Four years ago, the family had resisted an attempt by Annabelle's aunt to acquire custody of her, and she was now an unofficial Enright, dividing her time between Jack and Esther's home in Watford during the school terms and the senior Enright house in Hackney during the holidays. The mid-term break ended this coming Friday, and Percy was already dreading having to escort her back to Watford. He knew that his wife, Beatrice, felt the same and would cry buckets all the way home after bidding her goodbye for another school term.

'Captain Biggins is happy to come ashore after his long voyage to the Bahamas,' Annabelle announced, and Percy marvelled yet again at the depth of the girl's imagination. She spent most of her leisure hours writing stories, which she would read to Percy and Beattie in front of the fire in the sitting room.

'That vessel has seen many a journey over the years,' Percy smiled as he nodded towards the simple sailing boat that he'd made for his nephew Jack, then only fourteen years old. He'd shared their home until he'd followed Percy's lead and joined the Metropolitan Police, taking a room of his own in Whitechapel, around the corner from the old Leman Street police station.

'Is it true that Uncle Jack once sailed this boat?' Annabelle asked as she tucked it under the arm of her smock.

'Yes, he did,' Percy smiled as the memories flooded back, 'except then it was captained by Admiral Nelson. Anyway, to judge by the lengthening of the sun's rays, it's time that we headed home for an early supper. Then you can read us your latest story.'

'It's not finished yet,' Annabelle insisted, 'and I need to go to the Chinese house, to ask how Peter and Polly managed to rid the land around it of that dragon.'

'Very well, but only for a few minutes,' Percy conceded. 'If I take you home after dark, your Aunt Beattie will hang me upside down.'

'Alongside that ham that's hanging in the scullery?' Annabelle quipped, then took off at high speed towards the Chinese Pagoda that was such a popular feature of Victoria Park.

A short while later, they crossed Victoria Park Road and made their way home. As Percy pushed open the front gate to allow Annabelle to walk up the path with her precious sailing boat under her arm, Beattie appeared on the doorstep.

'I'm not sure if installing that telephone device was a good thing or not,' she grumbled. 'That Mr Morgan called yet again, complaining that you still haven't contacted him. That's three days in a row.'

'Didn't you tell him that my confidential enquiry business was temporarily suspended while we ensure that Annabelle gets the most out of her holiday? And didn't I also ask you to ask him to leave a message with Rufus Tomkins in my business office, so that I can decide whether or not I want to take on his case, whatever it may be about?'

'Of *course* I did, but he somehow got hold of our house number. He insists that if you don't visit him, he'll visit you. We're in no position to entertain your grubby little clients while Annabelle's staying with us. And in any case, Lucy also phoned, and I think you'll need to give her priority.'

'Our niece?' Percy asked.

'How many *other* women called Lucy do you know?'

'None, so far as I can recall. What did she want, anyway? Is Teddy looking for a subtle investigation into the business affairs of a professional rival?'

'No. In fact, this is probably more up your street — she insists that she's under suspicion of murder, and she sounded pretty hysterical.'

The following Sunday, both branches of the Enright family were gathered solemnly in the sitting room of Jack and Esther's house in Watford, where they lived with their four natural children. Percy and Beattie were due to return Annabelle, their 'adopted' fifth child, after they'd all had lunch together. While they waited for the food to be prepared, they were discussing Lucy's plight.

'So you haven't actually been charged yet?' Jack asked his sister solicitously.

Lucy shook her head, on the verge of tears as she gulped down a much-needed mouthful from her second gin and tonic.

'Then what makes you think that you will?' Percy asked.

Lucy shuddered as she replied, 'All the evidence seems to point to me, and that horribly cold Inspector Buxton clearly has grave suspicions. I can't honestly blame him, because *I'd* think I was guilty on the facts he's got. I didn't do it, I *swear*, but you've got to help me — *please!*'

The two male Enrights were well placed to assess the case against Lucy, and do what they could to find alternatives. Percy had retired after forty years in the Met, having achieved the rank of Inspector, while Jack was already a Chief Inspector at Scotland Yard. The section he currently led was Recruitment and Manpower, but before that he'd had years of hands-on experience in crime-fighting, and he and Percy had solved many a crime with a combination of Jack's dogged perseverance and Percy's talent for bending the rules to breaking point.

'You need to tell us every little detail that might have a bearing on the case,' Percy insisted as Esther refreshed his whisky and soda, knowing that once well lubricated with his favourite tipple, Percy could be persuaded to bring his experience and analytical skills to bear on the knottiest problem. Not that Esther lacked a clear brain herself when it came to the application of logic. More than once in the past, her husband and his uncle had asked for her insight, which subsequently had proved crucial in the solving of a case.

'Well,' Lucy began, 'we were staging *Julius Caesar* in our theatre, and it was the final night of our run. I don't know how well you know the classics, but at the start of Act Three, immediately after an interval of ten minutes, the main character — who's obviously Caesar himself — is assassinated by a group of five conspirators, who stab him to death in the Capitol. That was like the main Parliament building in Rome at the time.'

'Here endeth the ancient history lesson,' Beattie muttered. 'I'll just go and see if Polly could use a hand in the kitchen.'

'We can only hope that Polly doesn't let her near the food,' said Percy as the door closed behind her. 'I was *so* looking forward to a cow that was dead, but not actually cremated. Sorry, go on, Lucy.'

'Well,' she continued, 'staging an assassination obviously entails a good deal of direction. I was doing just about everything this time, given our falling volunteer numbers — producing, directing and acting as stage manager and props manager. That's what got me into this mess, of course.'

'Props?' Percy prompted her.

'They're the physical things that go on stage, like items of furniture, drinks glasses, and weapons,' Lucy explained. 'In this case, a set of five theatrical daggers.'

'How do they differ from real ones?' Jack asked. 'This is presumably how someone got stabbed to death?'

'That's *precisely* what happened,' Lucy said with a shudder. 'There were five conspirators — assassins, if you prefer — and they'd each been issued with a theatrical dagger with which to stab Caesar. The stage direction was for them to huddle round him in a group, and for the dagger blades coming in from behind Caesar to be wielded high in the air before being brought down in a stabbing motion, so that a tracker spot — that's a spotlight — could catch them glinting. Then the conspirators at the front — who obviously had their backs to the audience — were to stab inwards, towards Caesar, who was then to utter the immortal line, "Et tu Brute? Then fall Caesar," before doing precisely that. I knew something was wrong when he failed to utter the line. Then the actors leapt back from his corpse in horror when they realised that he'd *really* been stabbed.'

'You need to tell us exactly how you set about preventing that,' Percy insisted. 'I assume that the daggers are some sort of conjuring piece?'

'Yes, you're right,' Lucy confirmed. 'They're made from steel, and they have a spring device in the handle that forces the blade to retract into it when the point of it meets the slightest resistance. These devices are almost as old as Shakespeare's theatre, and I've never heard of a case when they "misfired", as it were. But on this occasion, and for a reason that we'll come to in a moment, one of the daggers failed to retract, and the actor playing Caesar received a fatal blow to the chest, somewhere around the heart, apparently. There was a lot of blood, anyway.'

'Are these daggers checked before the actors are issued with them?' Esther asked.

Lucy nodded. 'Obviously, because if the hinge mechanism becomes rusted, or perhaps even just damp, then the blade is at risk of not retracting. But that's not what happened here, seemingly.'

'Well, what *did* happen, and why are you suspected of *making* it happen?' Percy asked.

'I was in charge of those damned things. As props manager, it was my job to make the weapons available, and make sure that they were safe to handle, so that the blades would retract when they hit their target. I obviously did that, and I left the five daggers on the props table for the actors to pick up as they went on stage. I swear that they were all working perfectly when I left them.' The colour left Lucy's face. 'It turned out that the dagger that killed the actor had a piece of metal jammed up the side of the blade, where it joined the hilt, preventing the blade from retracting as it was meant to do.'

'What sort of metal?' Esther asked.

Lucy burst into tears as she replied, 'One of my hatpins!'

Lucy's husband Teddy put his arms around her, and she sobbed uncontrollably for a few minutes, while everyone sat staring at each other in embarrassment. Lucy had always been a model of cool self-control, a perfect society hostess, and the last person to give way to emotion.

It finally felt silent, and Percy took the opportunity to observe, 'A hatpin, you say? Why can it be alleged that it was yours?'

'I foolishly admitted it when they showed it to me,' Lucy confessed, then looked with reddened eyes towards Esther. 'You remember how proud my mother was of her hatpin collection?'

'Yes, of course,' Esther replied sadly, 'and she left it to you in her will, because you always admired them greatly, and you tend to wear fancy hats that can blow off in a stiff breeze unless they're fixed to your hair.'

'Well,' Lucy continued, 'several of them are *very* distinctive, and one in particular I always wore as a sort of good luck charm — the one with the red crown on its head, if you remember it. When Inspector Buxton showed it to me, and asked if I'd ever seen it before, I told him that it was one of mine, and easily recognisable. It was then that he told me that it had been used to jam the knife blade in order to make it fatal when used.'

'Several points, if I may,' Percy responded. 'First of all, if you were the guilty party, you'd be very unlikely to admit to the hatpin being yours. Secondly, even *if* it was used to jam the knife blade, that doesn't mean that you did it. And finally, who else could have had access to both the knives and the hatpin at the same time?'

'I've obviously been giving that a great deal of thought, and I can't positively eliminate any of the others in the Holborn Players who were there for that performance.'

'The motive for the killing may well have been a personal one, either a hatred of the victim, or to get back at you for some reason from the past,' said Jack. 'By looking at who might have wanted this actor dead, or you looking like a murderer, we may get you off the hook. If you're on it in the first place, that is. What makes you think that this Inspector Buxton suspects you?'

Lucy grimaced. 'Apart from the fact that I had access to all the daggers, and the opportunity to sabotage one of them?'

'Both of those facts are purely circumstantial,' Percy countered. 'They do, however, make it more possible that there was a second target — namely you. Was there someone in your company with a burning resentment against *both* of you?'

'That's where it gets worse, in a sense,' Lucy replied glumly, 'and adds to the reasons why I'm currently Inspector Buxton's first choice as the culprit. During rehearsals for Julius Caesar, I had a massive row with the actor in the title role — an old tosspot called Valentine Primrose. The one who was murdered.'

'Tell us more about that,' Percy requested with a frown.

'Well, he can — sorry, *could* — be an old woman at the best of times, and during rehearsals he objected to a particular scene earlier on in the play, when I wanted him to display more arrogance, and he wanted to play for sympathy. He challenged my authority and ability as a director, and I called him a simpering old fool. He went into a screaming rage and threatened to call a meeting of the trustees of the theatre group and have me sacked as director. I wasn't feeling my best that day, and told him that he'd live to regret it if he did. I didn't mean anything other than the fact that if it wasn't for my faith in him as an actor, he wouldn't be getting as many lead parts as he did. But everyone was on stage at the time, and when they were being interviewed by Buxton, one of them must have reported it, and you can see how it might be misinterpreted. As it transpired, so far as I know, he never did lodge a complaint, but even so it gives me a motive, doesn't it? And isn't that what police look for when they're investigating a case?'

Jack sighed and muttered, '"Means, motive, opportunity" — that's what they're taught when they first start in the Detective Branch, I'm afraid.'

'And in many cases they're wrong!' Percy insisted heatedly. 'How could *anyone* who knows Lucy suspect for one moment that she's capable of murder?'

'They *don't* know her like we do, and Buxton's obviously put the blinkers on,' said Jack. 'You know how it goes, Uncle Percy — identify a likely suspect, then make the facts fit. Put on the blindfold and go for a conviction.'

'That's only how the bad ones work,' Percy reminded him, 'and that's why I was so unpopular with the big hats in the Yard, when I went against conventional thinking. We need to unstitch the facts and look at them a different way. Let's start by getting as much information as we can from Lucy about all the other actors and stagehands who were there at the time. Who had the opportunity and the means, first of all, then the more difficult matter of motive.'

'So you'll help me?' Lucy asked pleadingly.

Percy nodded. 'Did you ever doubt it? If you can't help family, then you've no business calling yourself an investigator.'

'And you're my little sister,' Jack reminded her, 'so count me in as well.'

'I'll never forget how you brought Jack and me back together again after we'd had our first lovers' tiff,' Esther said with a smile. 'So insofar as I can be of any use, I'll do my bit as well.'

'I was hoping you'd say that,' said Percy, 'because despite his usefulness in practical matters, Jack doesn't have your ability to think sideways, and examine a case from more than one angle. We'll start with a list of all other potential candidates, and turn them inside out for motive.'

After lunch, the children were allowed to go to Cassiobury Park to work off some excess energy under the stern eye of Aunt Beattie. Meanwhile, Lucy, Jack, Percy and Esther reconvened with pots of tea in the sitting room, and Lucy began elaborating on the scribbled note she'd compiled on a dinner napkin during the meal.

'Let's begin with the man who on the surface was the most obvious culprit — Leo Carter. He was the one who had the fatal knife in his hand,' she reminded them.

'And therefore the least likely to have done it,' Percy observed. 'He'd be too obvious a suspect, although again we should perhaps consider him a victim. Perhaps the real offender had a reason for pointing the finger of suspicion in his direction.'

'You're forgetting that the daggers were all just lying on the table, waiting to be picked up at random by the actors playing the conspirator parts, before they went on stage,' Lucy pointed out. 'How could the real killer be sure that Leo would pick up the very knife that had been tampered with?'

'We'll come back to that question later,' Percy insisted. 'Tell us about this Carter character anyway, bearing in mind that anything — anything, mind — that you can tell me about him will make it easier for me to start a more thorough investigation of his background, character and possible motive.'

'Well,' Lucy began, 'he's in his early forties, so far as I can tell, and he's a schoolmaster at a private school down the road from us in St Paul's. I think he teaches the classics or something to senior boys. I remember, when we first started rehearsing *Julius Caesar*, that he'd would launch into boring lectures on the real history of that period, until Ernest Graves told him to "cease your prattle, sweetie, because you're driving us daft." I think his use of "sweetie" was a reference to Leo's tendency to be a bit effeminate in his manner.'

'And what about the deceased?' Percy asked. 'Was *he* also effeminate in his manner?'

'He could be, sometimes, why?'

'Well, he might have had some connection with Carter that wasn't entirely theatrical,' Percy replied.

'I doubt it. Leo was one of our most experienced and able actors, and he and Val — the deceased — regularly vied with each other for the lead roles in our productions.'

'That makes him a potential suspect, of course,' Jack pointed out.

Percy nodded. 'Anything else you can tell us about Carter?' he asked Lucy.

'I think he's divorced, but I'm not sure. Apart from that, nothing.'

'Very well. Tell us as much as you can about the others.'

'Well,' Lucy continued, 'there was Simon Abelman, a barrister who lives in Grays Inn Road somewhere. He's sort of "radical", if you know what I mean, and his lady friend's a total horror. Always going on about the role of women in society, and how much better it would be if women were given a greater hand in running it. She approved of me, of course, given my status in the theatre company, but for a while I think she was suspicious that I might be trying to steal Simon from her. Me, a woman approaching forty, respectably married and with three children! However, I think I managed to disabuse her of that notion. Sorry, you were asking about Simon. Well, he's an excellent actor, if a bit pompous. He got up Inspector Buxton's nose when he objected to his callous attitude towards poor Leo, who was a total mess after Val's death, although of course it was his hand that had caused it, albeit innocently.'

'We don't know that yet,' Percy reminded her, 'and if he's a good enough actor to be in your company, then he could have been faking his grief.'

'Somehow I doubt it,' Lucy replied. 'Anyway, that's about all I can tell you about Simon. Except that he's Jewish, if that has any bearing on the situation.'

'I sincerely hope not,' Esther muttered. 'There was a time when those of us from that community were blamed for everything, particularly in the East End, but that disgusting and totally unwarranted generalisation seems, in recent years, to have passed on to more recent immigrant groups — particularly the Russians, although many of those are also Jewish. That seems to be overlooked, which is perhaps as well, given that my grandparents also came from there originally.'

'I think we should let Lucy continue, dearest,' Jack told her gently.

Esther nodded. 'Sorry, everyone — I'm now off my soapbox, but I may say, as a final point, that a Jewish man with a lady friend who's interested in women's rights might well have had a motive to make a point of some sort. What exactly, I don't know, but that's my tuppence worth.'

'And well worth keeping in mind,' Percy replied with a smile. 'Now, Lucy — who else?'

'Well, there's Arthur Dennistoun. He's an art dealer with business premises in the West End somewhere. He's frightfully rich, but not a particularly gifted actor. To be perfectly honest, he sort of bought his way into our theatre group by making a very generous contribution during one of our earlier funding appeals. Amateur theatres like ours depend on rich patrons, as you're probably aware.'

'Anyone else?' Percy asked.

'Talking of old money, there's Henry Gloucester, a bit of a "dandy", or so he'd like to think. A string of broken romances behind him, and always impeccably turned out. His money comes from his medical practice in Marylebone somewhere, specialising in "ladies' problems". Mind you, if you ask me, the ladies' problems are only just beginning when they meet Henry Gloucester, with his oozing charm, what he no doubt regards as his "rakish" demeanour, and of course his money.'

'Have we accounted for them all?' Percy asked as he looked up from the notes he'd been making.

'There's one more, if we're concentrating, at this stage, on the actors who were involved in the assassination scene,' Lucy told him. 'The most recent addition to the company, and a fine actor. We were lucky to get him, because according to him he was being considered by two other theatre companies in central London. Ours was the most convenient for where he lives in Theobalds Road, apparently, so he favoured us with his undoubted acting talents.'

'Name?' Percy prompted her.

'His name is Ernest Graves, and he works in some Government office or other in Whitehall. Not sure which, or what he does there, but he's been very eager to impress upon me that it's important, and something to do with the Navy. And that's the lot — for the leading actors, anyway. As for the rest of the cast and the stagehands, I'd need to go back into my records to give you a complete list.'

'No, I think we have more than enough to proceed with already,' said Percy. 'Jack and I will start work immediately.'

'We will?' Jack asked. 'Apart from the existing onerous demands on my working hours, what did you have in mind, precisely?'

'You presumably have access to criminal records?'

'Naturally.'

'And you can get a copy of the existing file on the alleged murder of Valentine Primrose?'

'I can try, of course, but someone might want to know why.'

'Make Valentine Primrose's criminal history your first priority. If he has one, you can always claim to be assisting E Division in their enquiries.'

'Who'd be likely to believe that?' Jack asked disbelievingly.

Percy chuckled. 'You'd be surprised what the top brass in the Yard will accept if you sound sincere enough. But good luck, anyway. Now, it's time that I took a turn around the park with my pipe. I might even join Beattie and the children, just to spoil her afternoon.'

CHAPTER THREE

'Have you begun recruiting surgeons and art dealers into the Met?' asked Chief Superintendent Barrymore as he looked up from behind the desk in his third-floor office in the Scotland Yard headquarters building, to which Jack had been summoned. Barrymore was Jack's ultimate superior and inclined towards a hands-on role at the head of the section of the Yard for which he was responsible. He'd enjoyed a long and illustrious career as a 'villain-catcher' and found administrative work both tedious and unsatisfying. Particularly the likes of Recruitment and Manpower, of which Jack had been the head for some five years now.

Jack had been expecting this challenge, and was not sure that he could bluff his way out of it.

'Why do you ask, sir?' he attempted.

Barrymore snorted as he pointedly refrained from inviting Jack to take a seat. 'I should have thought that was bloody obvious, Enright!' he snarled. 'You've made five criminal history requests in the past three days, and one of them was in respect of a leading criminal barrister. I'm told that you were recruited into your current position because of your middle-class origins, in the belief that you'd attract like-minded chaps into the Met, but you're surely aiming too high with *this* lot, wouldn't you say?'

'They were all associated with a man called Valentine Primrose, who was murdered last week,' Jack replied, 'and I was interested to learn if any of them had a criminal background.'

'That's surely a matter for whoever's investigating that murder,' Barrymore pointed out, 'but it might explain why you also called for a copy of that file from E Division. I was going to enquire about that, too. So why are you diverting your recruitment efforts into this particular matter? Bored, are we?'

'No, sir — it's my sister.'

It fell icily silent, then Barrymore asked, 'What precisely is your sister's interest in the matter? And are you conducting your own enquiries on the side into a matter that's surely being handled competently by — let me see now…' He looked down at something on his desk. 'Yes, here it is — Inspector Buxton. So what's your sister got to do with this?'

'She was there when it happened,' Jack admitted. 'It's a long and complicated story, but she's fearful that she may have become a suspect, given the circumstances.'

'And so *you* were looking for other suspects, is that it?' Barrymore demanded as his face reddened. 'Interfering with an ongoing enquiry in the hope of getting her off the hook? If so, then I think you can anticipate what I'm going to say next.'

'I think I can guess the general nature of it, sir,' Jack all but whispered.

'You're to have nothing more to do with this case. You're to return all those papers to Records without delay, and get back to your normal duties. Is that understood?'

'Yes, sir,' Jack replied meekly, then turned to go.

Barrymore called him back with a less aggressive facial expression, then told him, 'I hear good reports of your work wherever I enquire, Enright, and your recruitment statistics in recent months have been excellent. Don't blow your career with this, understood?'

'Yes, sir,' Jack repeated, and this time he was allowed to leave.

Back in the sanctity of his own office, he made an urgent telephone call to Uncle Percy at home.

'Tang Li's Chophouse at noon,' he instructed him, 'if you want this information I've got for you. Bring a pencil and a good supply of paper, because you'll be doing a lot of copying.'

'Will I be allowed to eat as well?' Percy asked.

'Provided that you don't get food all over your notes,' Jack replied. 'This is your only chance to see what I've got before I have to hand it back.'

'So why are you in such a hurry to give me this stuff, and why do I have to make notes?' Percy demanded as he gave his meat pie order to the waiter in their favourite lunch establishment on the Embankment.

'Because I have to hand everything back "without delay", to use Chief Superintendent Barrymore's exact words,' Jack told him as he pointed to the chicken chow mien on the handwritten menu card. 'All but one of them are as clean as a whistle, although there was an allegation two years or so ago that Dennistoun — he's the art dealer — was guilty of a fraud, substituting a fake for a masterpiece. He managed to persuade a jury that the fake was so good that even he was fooled, so had no dishonest intent. At least, if you scribble hard enough, you'll have all their home addresses at the time that I conducted the search. I'd be willing to bet that your average ratepayer in London has no idea that we keep records of even those who've never transgressed. In addition, of course, you've got the report of the Primrose murder as viewed by Buxton, and he certainly seems to be suspicious of Lucy.'

'No wonder, to judge by what she told us on Sunday, and what Buxton's noted here,' Percy muttered. 'If I'd been handed this ten years ago, I'd probably have arrested her by now. So the sooner I begin investigating the rest of them, the better.'

'How do you intend to set about it?' Jack asked.

Percy winked conspiratorially. 'Presumably Lucy's theatre group — or at least the landlords of the building that they're renting — have taken out an insurance policy against fire or something. Even if they haven't, the actors won't know that, and it will be a plausible cover for me to interview each of them for their memory of what actually happened. When the inconsistencies begin to emerge, then we'll know where to probe next.'

'We? Didn't I just tell you that I've been warned off the case?'

'Yes, but you're an Enright. Enrights never take "no" for an answer, and the person whose neck we're setting out to save is also an Enright, at least by birth. And I've no doubt that Esther will wish to bring her cool logical brain to bear on any seeming conundrum.'

'But what exactly do you think I'll be able to contribute?'

'I'll let you know that when I know. Now, I've got all I need from these papers, so take them back to the Yard like a good boy, and let's enjoy the lunch that appears to be heading our way.'

Percy Enright smiled at the prospect of a new puzzle to solve, and one that would involve the entire family, one way or the other, as he turned the corner of Mare Street, Hackney and began walking north along it, towards the side-street in which his professional office was located above a candle shop. Given that the route he was taking was along one of the main thoroughfares in the suburb, he was enjoying the luxury of walking up a designated pedestrian pavement, and did not need to take steps to avoid the seemingly empty horse bus that was plodding down towards him in the opposite direction. All he had to do was walk to one side of the two burly men who seemed to be keeping pace with the horse bus.

Then, as it drew abreast of him, each of the two men grabbed one of his arms and lifted him bodily, turning in a well-choreographed move to throw him onto the bus platform, where other eager arms dragged him inside. The bus suddenly increased its speed as the driver applied the whip to the horse's rear end, and turned right into a series of narrow side streets. Percy looked up from where he'd landed on the floor into the barrel of a revolver being wielded by a stern-faced man.

'Don't look so surprised, Mr Enright,' the man smiled coldly. 'Mr Morgan is not a man to be ignored, and you *were*, after all, invited to meet with him. You were also warned that if necessary he would come to you, although due to the pressure of other commitments it turns out that we have to take *you* to *him*. If you promise to behave yourself, and if you believe that I will not hesitate to fire several shots into your lower torso should you offer any resistance, then you may take a seat and enjoy the ride.'

'The ride to *where*, precisely? Who are you, why have I been abducted like this, and how did you know that today was the first day that I had intended to visit my business premises this week?'

The man smiled. 'Mr Morgan is persistent, and your employee obligingly told him that you would be attending your office in Devonshire Road this morning. As for your remaining questions, my precise identity is entirely irrelevant, and if you look out of the window you may recognise parts of the neighbouring suburb of Dalston. Our ultimate destination is in Holloway — Tufnell Park Road, to be precise.'

'Where I will meet Mr Morgan?'

'You will indeed, along with others, all of whom share an interest in securing your services.'

'For what, precisely?'

'One question too many, Mr Enright. Even if I knew the answer, it would not be part of my limited role to disclose it. Now, sit back and enjoy the delights of North London.'

The journey was no more comfortable than any other on a horse bus that rattled and swayed its way through street after street. It had a sign on its front indicating that it was not in service, so no-one was inclined to put out their hand as they slowly progressed through one suburb after another.

Eventually they were heading north on Holloway Road, and Percy had just recognised its junction with Seven Sisters Road when the vehicle turned left into Tufnell Park Road and proceeded down it until it came to a stylish house set back in its own grounds. There the bus came to a halt. Percy was ordered out at gunpoint, and was prodded up the front drive to a two-storey, flat-roofed late Georgian dwelling. The front door opened from the inside as they approached it.

Further prodding from the revolver in his back urged Percy down a short hallway on the ground floor, from which four rooms led off. They came to the second door on the right, just before what appeared to be a kitchen, and the man with the weapon reached around in front of Percy and opened it. A final prod obliged Percy to enter the room, where a man sat in an armchair and gave Percy a broad smile.

'Mr Morgan, I presume?' Percy asked.

'No, my name's Vernon Kell,' the man replied, 'but Mr Morgan will join us without delay, once he's told that you're finally here. Please take the obvious seat.'

There was another comfortable chair opposite Kell's, and Percy did as instructed.

Kell smiled and asked, 'Now that we're both sitting comfortably, what do you know about a Government department known as MO Three?'

'Absolutely nothing,' Percy admitted, 'but presumably you'll be advising me all about it before I'm allowed to leave — assuming that I ever am, although if you'd simply brought me here in order to do away with me you'd have been wasting a good deal of time and manpower. A simple shot from a rooftop would have sufficed, and may I assume that my services are required yet again by a Government from which I retired several years ago?'

'One never retires from service to the Government, Percy, as you must appreciate,' said Kell. 'Take myself, for example. I was employed to do valuable work for the Foreign Office in China, and returned after what was described as "exemplary service" three years ago, hoping to return to my native Norfolk in order to enjoy a retirement of sorts. Then some busybody in the War Office took it into his head that I might be of value analysing intelligence coming out of Germany, with which we enjoy, if that is the appropriate word, a somewhat tense relationship at present, due to Kaiser Wilhelm's antipathy towards his uncle, our dear King Edward. You became aware of that, of course, while investigating that murder in Buckinghamshire a few years ago, for which the Kaiser tried to blame Prince Bertie. You and your nephew Jackson proved particularly valuable in that, and now that I've been obliged to lead a new undercover bureau within the War Office known as MO Three, I naturally thought of you.'

'And what makes you think that I'd want to work with either you *or* the War Office?' Percy demanded. 'For one thing I've got better things to do, and for another I didn't exactly enjoy my previous encounters with your political masters.'

'You won't be working *with* me,' Kell replied coldly, 'since I'm several grades above your level of operation. What you'll be engaged with is much closer to street level, and involves the kind of grubby underhand snooping in which you excel, or so I'm told by those who know you better, and have recommended you for the job.'

'So I'll be working alone, assuming that I accept?' Percy asked.

Kell sighed. 'Any right you had to refuse evaporated once I advised you of the existence of MO Three. But you won't exactly be working alone, nor will your reports be consigned to some box on a lonely moor in the middle of nowhere. This house is the centre of MO3 information collection — a kind of suburban post box, if you prefer — and it's managed by a former colleague of yours, who calls himself William Morgan.'

'So I've already met him?' Percy asked unnecessarily. 'If so, then why did I not recognise the name?'

'Because it's not his real name, and he seemed to think that you'd refuse to have anything to with MO Three if you knew that real name. That was, of course, while you still had a choice in the matter.'

Percy frowned. 'So when *do* I get to meet the mysterious Mr Morgan?'

'One moment,' Kell said as he reached for the small handbell on the table alongside it, and rang it five times. The door opened, and Percy turned in his chair, then leapt to his feet when he recognised the man who'd just entered.

'I might have known it!' Percy shouted. 'I thought I'd seen the last of William Melville!'

CHAPTER FOUR

'Hello, Percy,' Melville said with a smile. 'I know what you're about to say, and I know what you're thinking, but we're no longer serving together in the Met, and I'm no longer the superintendent in charge of Special Branch. This means that I no longer have to maintain a disciplinary distance between us, and even you would have to admit that you were the greatest nightmare any senior officer ever had to face. Arrogant, swift to take offence, disobedient and a persistent rule-breaker. And those were your good features.'

'And you were a pompous, miserable old bastard who lived off my results,' Percy snarled. 'You'll pardon me if I don't mention your good features, because I don't recall any, and I'm not given to idle flattery.'

'Well,' Kell said as silence descended, 'now that we're all re-acquainted, let's see what we can do, collectively, in England's cause, shall we? Percy's been left in no doubt that he has no choice in the matter, but hopefully what William has to tell him will make him more enthusiastic.'

'I can't think of anything that might achieve that,' Percy grumbled, 'except perhaps a free account at a top restaurant.'

'You really haven't changed, even though you've now become a grandfather of sorts,' Melville observed.

Percy shot him a glare. 'Leave Annabelle out of this!' he thundered.

'William meant no harm by that, Percy,' Kell hastened to assure him. 'It's just that we were keeping an eye on you for future recruitment. Which is why we knew that the time was right, given your niece Lucy's current … "difficulty", shall we say?'

'And you're about to offer to make that difficulty go away if I co-operate, is that it?' Percy demanded.

'No, Percy — *you're* going to make it go away, by your own efforts, when you follow up the leads that we're about to give you,' Kell replied. 'And I think that we could all benefit from tea and cakes at this point in our newfound relationship.'

Percy was on his third slice of cake when Melville made a confession.

'Believe me when I assure you that it really went against the grain to have to appear to be disciplining you during our Yard days, Percy,' he said. 'You were, and no doubt still are, a man after my own heart, when it comes to bringing wrongdoers to heel. But I couldn't be seen to condone your constant failure to follow the correct procedures, always cocking a snook at authority and using underhand methods to bring your quarry to heel. The very qualities that we need you for now, and I hope that we can become closer friends in the process.'

'If you'd said something along those lines five years ago, I wouldn't have been so abrasive in my manner towards you,' Percy admitted, 'but you really *did* come across as a pompous old fool, never acknowledging the skill that went into being as devious as I could be at times.'

'So we can work together in harmony?' Melville asked as he held out a hand.

Percy nodded as he reached out to grasp it. 'So what's involved?' he asked. 'And what has it to do with my niece Lucy?'

Melville looked across the tea table for confirmation from Kell, who nodded, then Melville asked Percy, 'Did Lucy give you the names of those who were in her theatre company at the time of the undoubted murder of Primrose?'

'The names of the main actors who took part in the assassination scene, certainly,' Percy confirmed.

'And was one of them called "Graves"?'

'The name strikes a chord,' Percy conceded guardedly.

Kell took over the briefing. 'Ernest Graves is employed as a cipher clerk in the Admiralty, in which capacity he's regularly required to send coded signals to English naval bases, from which they can relay them to our warships. In recent months, our troopships going about their lawful purposes on the high seas have been dogged by German vessels, disguised to look like freighters, but in fact known to be part of the Kaiser's Imperial German Navy. They always seem to know where we are, and we suspect that this is the result of someone giving them knowledge of the sailing orders conveyed through Graves's ciphers. We also have reason to believe that the Germans have got the plans of a new and more powerful battleship that we've been developing in our Portsmouth dockyard. It's called the *Dreadnought*, and it will outgun anything the Germans have at present, but our spies tell us that a new keel has just been laid in the ironically named Kiel shipyard in Germany that has all the hallmarks of *Dreadnought*. Those plans were kept in a secure vault within the Admiralty that could only be accessed by those with appropriate security clearance, which Graves clearly has, given his cipher duties.'

'But even so, he could hardly just walk in there and say, "Show me the *Dreadnought* plans," I presume?' Percy asked.

For the first time that morning, Kell looked embarrassed. 'We believe that he may have prevailed upon another clerk who worked inside the vault to lend him a security key for long enough for him to access what he needed. When I say "prevail", I really mean "blackmail", in return for not revealing their sexual indiscretions. Indiscretions to which Graves was a party.'

'He seduced her, you mean?' Percy said with a smile. 'She wouldn't be the first to be seduced, and I assume that she had a husband somewhere in the background, or parents who would be disapproving of her loss of honour, hence the threat to reveal "indiscretions". Why are you looking so coy about it?'

'Better tell him the whole story, Vernon,' Melville suggested, 'if you want him working at his best, that is.'

'Well,' Kell replied in a low voice, 'you should know that the clerk whose indiscretions I'm referring to is male — name of Mark Adlington, who we obviously never suspected of being that way inclined. He's "homosexual", to use the polite word for it. We obviously look very closely into a person's background before they're recruited to work in sensitive Government areas, and this one must have slipped under the wire, to adopt a horseracing term with which we know you're very familiar. And, of course, were his true inclinations to be revealed, he'd be out of a job, which is why Graves was able to use blackmail.'

'But this Adlington chap can't have been the only one to "slip under the wire", as you put it,' Percy pointed out. 'May we assume that Graves is "inclined" the same way?'

'We don't know that for certain,' Kell replied, 'which is why we need you to conduct undercover enquiries.'

'You want me to pretend to be like him?' Percy asked incredulously. 'A man in his mid-sixties, happily married, with no previous indication of such a preference? I don't think that would be my best undercover guise, and you must be desperate to even suggest it.'

'That's not what we're suggesting, Percy,' Melville assured him. 'We had in mind something more along the lines of you discovering whether or not he was involved in that murder in the theatre that your niece is suspected of. We were thinking of inviting you aboard long before that man Primrose got himself stabbed, but when we realised who Lucy Masefield's uncle was, well, you just fell neatly into the picture. If we can prove that he killed Primrose, then we're relieved of any need to prove his homosexual inclinations as the reason for removing him from a position in which he can prejudice the nation's security.'

'But do we know of any reason why Graves would want Primrose dead?' asked Percy.

'All we know is that Primrose was a frequenter of molly houses,' Kell told him, 'so there's the possible connection. If Graves's possible preferences became known to Primrose, who realised the potential for blackmail given Graves's Government position, then there's your motive.'

'And all I need are the means and opportunity,' said Percy with a frown. 'It comes down to working out who could possibly have put the fatal weapon in the hands of that innocent dupe Carter.'

'Which you were planning on doing anyway, were you not, in order to absolve your niece of any blame?' Melville reminded him. 'Our paths have crossed neatly, Percy. But there's another matter we want you to look into while you're about it.'

Percy sighed. 'You want me to investigate Harry Houdini and have him charged with fraud, perhaps?'

It was Kell's turn to sigh. 'Please take this more seriously, for God's sake. We're offering you a second opportunity to unmask whoever may have been behind the murder of Primrose, but first we need to give you a little more information about the running of MO Three. Only as much as you need to perform your allotted task more efficiently, mind.'

'I was under the obviously false impression that it was only *one* task,' Percy replied crossly. 'Find out who murdered Primrose, and why.'

'Essentially that's true,' Kell agreed, 'but you'll be coming at it from two different directions, and will need to be aware of how MO Three works.'

'I already know that,' Percy muttered. 'It pulls law-abiding citizens off the street and forces them to eat cake while selling their soul to some sort of clandestine department working below the parapet of lawful behaviour.'

Kell chose to ignore this. 'MO Three works in two distinct halves,' he explained. 'I have ultimate responsibility for one half — the International Division, as we like to call it — while William here has control of the Domestic Division. The business involving Graves was obviously of primary concern to me, but William also has one of his own, which happily may also have implications for the murder of Primrose. Back to you, William.'

Melville looked into Percy's eyes and asked, 'Did Lucy ever mention a woman called "Florence Bannister", can you recall?'

'I *can* recall, and she didn't,' Percy insisted, so Melville tried again.

'Simon Abelman?'

'Yes, he was one of the actors playing the conspirators who murdered Caesar. He's a barrister with a clean criminal history — as of course it would need to be.'

'Well, Abelman has a lover called Florence Bannister,' Melville told him, 'and she's on our list of those being closely monitored for subversive activity with regard to all this "women's suffrage" nonsense.'

'I'm not one of those who believe it to be "nonsense", but carry on,' Percy replied.

Melville took a mouthful of tea, then launched into his explanation. 'First of all, allow me to deliver a short political history lesson. Two years ago, a group of well-meaning, respectable, middle-class ladies from Manchester formed an organisation that they called the Women's Social and Political Union, or WSPU for short. Their objective was to secure voting rights for women, and this new organisation grew out of the Independent Labour Party, one of whose members had been a firebrand radical barrister called Richard Pankhurst. He died in eighteen ninety-eight, but he left behind a widow, Emmeline, and five children, including two daughters called Christabel and Sylvia. It's these three women who established the WSPU two years ago. With me so far?'

'Of course,' said Percy, 'but I'm waiting eagerly to learn of its relevance to what you want me to do.'

'Bear with me. They began in a mild way, persuading a local Member of Parliament to introduce a Bill to give voting and other rights to women — what we may collectively call "suffrage rights". The Bill was talked out — indeed *laughed* out — only weeks ago, and the WSPU have, we believe, begun planning more direct action. By that I mean public demonstrations, heckling of politicians on platforms, and general disorder in the streets.'

'A bit like the so-called Match Girls some years ago, who gathered in large numbers in the park across from my house, then marched on Parliament, leading to controversial confrontations with officers from the Met?' Percy reminisced. 'I remember it well.'

'Good,' Melville replied, 'but what you may not recall are the names of those women who sought to make political capital out of what was basically a workplace complaint about working conditions. One of them was named Annie Besant, and she's one of this new WSPU lot. You can see where we're heading with all this?'

'You're apprehensive of more disorder?'

'Precisely. And another member of this newly emerged WSPU is Florence Bannister.'

'Who's the lover of Simon Abelman?'

'The very same, and *his* background gives us cause for concern as well,' said Melville. 'He's very left-wing, as they call it, in his political views, and the causes he chooses to defend are all in the general area of what you might politely call "social reform", but some would call "anarchistic overthrow of the established order". We're not sure whether or not his association with Florence Bannister came about naturally, given that he was for a while a disciple of Richard Pankhurst, or whether Bannister wormed her way into his emotions — and his bed — in an attempt to secure the services of a sympathetic lawyer when they start getting arrested for public disorder offences.'

'So it would also suit your ambitions to have this Simon Abelman convicted of the murder of Primrose? You're giving me another potential suspect to work on? But you can hardly expect me to unearth *two* murderers armed with *one* knife between them. And why would Abelman want Primrose dead?'

'No idea,' Melville replied, 'unless he'd learned something about revolutionary plans that Abelman was involved in. However, don't discount the possibility that Abelman and Graves were in it together, in which case we can perhaps buckle both of them in one go. But you can now perhaps appreciate how your interest in what happened when the Holborn Players staged *Julius Caesar* suddenly coincided with concerns that we had, and opened the door to your possible assistance.'

'And has Inspector Buxton been told to step back from his investigations into Lucy's possible involvement?' Percy asked. 'Or is that too much to hope for?'

'What do *you* think?' Kell put in. 'If you were in his position, during your days as an inspector from the Yard, and you were told by a Government department that you didn't even know existed to go slow on an investigation, what would have been your reaction?'

'I'd have pushed even harder,' Percy said with a grin, 'suspecting a whitewash.'

'Precisely,' Kell agreed, 'and we don't want any of those whom we suspect of involvement in the murder of Primrose to get any inkling of what we're about. More to the point, what *you're* about.'

'Are there any limits on my authority?' Percy asked, 'or am I free to do it in my own way?'

'We wouldn't have got you involved if we wanted "normal" investigative procedure,' Melville reminded him. 'You didn't play by the rules when you were bound by them, so why begin now? Just don't break the law in the process, that's all. Well, not seriously, anyway.'

'And how do I keep in touch?' was Percy's next question.

'You have the telephone installed, both in your home and your business premises,' said Kell, 'and we obviously have one here. But there's to be no operational detail discussed on the telephone, understood? We have reason to believe that the conversations that take place down those wires can be overheard by third parties, so only contact us via that method if you want to set up a meeting. Should you wish to do so, just ask for "a visit from Mr Morgan", and a coach or horse bus will await you outside your business premises in Devonshire Street within the hour. The same horse bus, probably, that will now take you back to where we intercepted you. Don't bother trying to speak with our operatives on that bus in order to acquire more information about MO Three — they're on loan from the armed forces, and they believe that our work is military in nature. They're also authorised to kill anyone who fails to comply with their instructions.'

'What a friendly organisation to work for,' Percy muttered as he rose to leave. 'But if it means that I can free my niece of any suspicion of murder, then I'm happy to join.'

'You still seem to believe that you had a choice,' Melville said, smiling coldly as he watched Percy heading for the door.

An hour later, Percy stepped off the empty bus and walked as far as The Mermaid in Mare Street, where he treated himself to a meat pie and a pint of best, before completing the walk to his office, where Rufus Tomkins raised both eyebrows in surprise.

'I was expecting you earlier this morning,' he complained, 'and I've run out of excuses to give to potential clients, most of whom have no doubt gone elsewhere. But Mrs Enright wasn't so easily fooled, and she called four times. I think she suspects you of something devious.'

'That's because she knows me too well,' Percy replied. 'I'm afraid I won't be available for new clients for the next week or two, but your wages are secure, so don't worry. If anybody asks, I'm engaged in mortal combat with aphids in my vegetable patch at home. See you in a fortnight or so.'

'I'm not allowed to tell you, and even if I did you wouldn't believe me,' Percy told his wife as he entered the house via the back scullery door, to find Beattie waiting for him with a question written across her face.

'I only had one question all day,' she replied tersely, 'and that was what you wanted for dinner.'

'Well, let me see now,' said Percy. 'So far today I've had several helpings of sponge cake and a meat pie, so perhaps one of your fish pies might be appropriate.'

'Lucy rang,' Beattie went on. 'She was hoping that you had some uplifting news for her.'

'In a sense, I do,' said Percy, 'and I believe that the time is right for another counsel of war in Watford. Could you prevail upon Esther to host it?'

'You're just hoping to get another beef roast, aren't you?' Beattie said crossly. 'You and your stomach have a lot to answer for.'

'Look at it this way,' said Percy. 'We'll get to see Annabelle again, and we might even emerge from it with a plan to keep our niece away from the hangman.'

CHAPTER FIVE

'I can't give you much detail,' Percy explained to the family the following Sunday. They were in Jack and Esther's sitting room, pre-lunch drinks in hand. 'But I *can* tell you that I have an official blessing to enquire unofficially, in my usual sneaky way, into how Valentine Primrose came to die, and — more to the point — at whose hand.'

'I know better than to enquire further into whatever authorisation Uncle Percy has,' Jack told them, 'and he probably won't even be allowed to tell me, but I think we're all about to be given a role to play. Except Aunt Beattie, of course, who'll be free to wage her undying campaign against wholesome cooking.'

They all laughed, and felt free to do so, since Beattie was out somewhere with the children.

'Those who have given their nod to my proceeding in my subversive fashion towards the discovery of the truth have indicated two possible leading suspects from the potential five that we began with,' Percy explained. 'They are Ernest Graves and Simon Abelman, both of them conspirators in the play, and both of them armed with knives at the time.'

'But not the fatal knife,' Lucy objected, 'and I wouldn't have picked either of those as likely suspects.'

'In my lengthy experience,' Percy went on, 'the least likely are the *most* likely, and the most suspicious-looking are usually the most innocent. Like you, of course, Lucy.'

'Point taken,' Lucy conceded. 'So what are your plans?'

'I'll obviously be ferreting through the backgrounds of both Graves and Abelman, before also enquiring into the recent histories of the remainder,' Percy replied. 'Jack has already discovered that the only one among them with any previous criminal stain on their copybook is Arthur Dennistoun, and that was only for an unproven fraud, so we begin with five "cleanskins", as they were known in my former trade. The first two of those on whom to turn the spotlight for motive are therefore Graves and Abelman, and those who instruct me have given me certain information that unfortunately I can't share, even with Jack. But that doesn't mean that I won't be relying on most of the rest of you to garner some additional intelligence on the movements of the "conspirators" immediately before the fatal stabbing.'

'And how do you propose that we do that?' Esther asked.

Percy turned to Lucy. 'Would you say that your older brother has any prospects as an actor?'

'I wouldn't have thought so, but if I anticipate what's coming next, you want me to pretend that he has?'

'Indeed. What's your next production, and is there a part in it for him?'

'We're soldiering on with the Shakespeare classics, despite the tragic outcome of the last one,' Lucy replied, 'and we hope to offer *Hamlet* some time before Christmas. I would imagine that my still youthful-looking brother could make an attempt of sorts at the role of Laertes, although given that he fights a duel to the death with Hamlet at the very end, I'll be guarding the fencing foils with *both* our lives.'

'Who is this "Lurtees" person, and what does he do, apart from getting killed?' Jack demanded.

'His name is Laertes,' Lucy corrected, 'and he's the brother of Ophelia, who's Hamlet's lady love. She commits suicide, Hamlet kills Laertes's father Polonius, and Laertes understandably gets very angry and challenges Hamlet to a duel, in which they both die, due to poison on the tips of their fencing blades. Basically you'd be playing the part of a young hothead, but Percy still has to explain why.'

'To me, in particular,' Jack agreed. 'So back to you, Uncle Percy.'

'I need someone inside the theatre, carefully watching how the other actors interact with each other.'

'Why can't I do that?' Lucy objected.

Percy smiled. 'Because you'll be helping Esther bang the drum for women's rights.'

'I was wondering if you'd have a role for me,' Esther put in, 'and I'm halfway there already.'

'So am I,' Lucy confirmed. 'As I already mentioned, Simon Abelman seemed particularly taken by my forthright views in that department, along with his somewhat prickly lady friend.'

'You refer to Florence Bannister, I take it?' Percy asked.

'Yes, her. And why do you need Esther in on this as well?'

'I want at least one of you to wangle an invitation to join something called the Women's Social and Political Union, or WSPU for short,' Percy told her. 'It's a new political organisation run *by* women, *for* women. Don't ask me why at this stage, but it's part of the deal I've done, to see if Simon Abelman had anything to do with Primrose's murder.'

'While I concentrate on Graves?' Jack asked.

Percy chuckled as he shook his head. 'I want you to observe the entire cast, not just one of them, then try to draw them out regarding their actions just before they went on stage on that fateful night. I take it that the same actors will be involved as in *Julius Caesar*?' he asked of Lucy, who nodded.

'By and large. We haven't held the final auditions yet, but *Hamlet* will almost certainly be played by Leo Carter, who is probably first in line for all the lead parts now that Val's dead.

A very good motive for him to have killed him, of course. Or it could be Ernest Graves. I had Simon Abelman down provisionally to play Laertes, and I think he'll prove to be very jealous of Jack if he gets the part. Polonius — Laertes's father, as I already mentioned — will probably be Arthur Dennistoun, while Henry Gloucester can be Claudius, Hamlet's uncle, and the real villain of the piece.'

'The wicked uncle,' Jack said with a smirk. 'Can't Uncle Percy play that part?'

'I'll be too busy doing other things behind the scenes, as it were,' Percy growled, 'but the key to what happened is how someone managed to manipulate the murder weapon into Leo Carter's hand. It may not necessarily have been intended that his would be the hand to strike the fatal blow, but we'll need to know if anyone was behaving suspiciously at the crucial moment when the actors picked up the knives and went on stage. Your enquiries will need to be subtle, Jack, which is not your strongest suit, but if you ask too many obvious questions, the real killer will get both suspicious and nervous, and we'll lose the vital opportunity to recreate what happened.'

'Let's hope that my abilities as an actor are more convincing than my powers of subtle enquiry,' Jack frowned, 'since you seem to have little faith in those.'

'You're the only one we can send in there with any credibility,' said Percy.

'Presumably not as "Jack Enright, Chief Inspector from Scotland Yard"?' Esther asked.

Percy shook his head. 'As usual, you're anticipating me. I thought perhaps "Jack Edwards", for several reasons. First of all, after almost forty years as brother and sister, it would be asking too much of Lucy not to call him "Jack", however careful she is. As for the "Edwards", that way we preserve the initials "J. E.", in case they show up in some context such as a monogrammed kerchief, or an item of jewellery.'

'You make me sound like some fop from Mayfair or Knightsbridge,' Jack complained, 'so what *is* my background, exactly?'

'I thought we might dream that up between us,' Percy replied. 'What's your background, where have you been all these years, why have you suddenly shown an interest in the theatre, and so on. You'll need to memorise your new life history thoroughly, so that there are no slip-ups. Lucy, is it unusual for someone of Jack's age to suddenly manifest an interest in the theatre?'

'Not at all,' said Lucy. 'In fact, most of those whom Jack will be mixing with — and in due course investigating — came to the Holborn Players later in life. I suggest that Jack sticks as closely as possible to what might have been his life if he hadn't joined the police force. You know — childhood in Barking, followed his father into insurance, has his own brokerage somewhere in the financial district, got bored with life after marriage and children, always had a hankering for life in front of the footlights, that sort of thing.'

'Excellent!' Percy enthused. 'You should take to writing plays yourself, Lucy.'

'Don't think I haven't tried,' she said with a smile. 'But how about you, Jack? Would you be comfortable with that assumed persona?'

'Certainly,' Jack agreed. 'Except for the bit about being bored with married life.'

'I was hoping you'd say that,' Esther murmured as she took his hand and kissed it. 'But what about me? I assume that I'll no longer be playing the part of Lucy's sister-in-law?'

'Why not?' said Percy. 'However, not by virtue of being married to her brother. How about being Teddy's sister-in-law instead? Would you have any objection to that, Teddy?'

'Obviously not,' Teddy replied, 'and I can give you a background story for her.'

'With respect,' Percy cautioned, 'and as Lucy rightly cautioned, we need to keep it as close to her real life story as possible. So she reverts to being Esther Isaacs, a Jewish-born orphan earning her living running a garment manufacturing business in Spitalfields, who met your fictitious brother Charles when she made a bespoke suit for him. Their romance blossomed, they were married over fifteen years ago, she has children by him as "Esther Masefield", and she began doing garment repair work for another theatre group. She has now joined the Holborn Players in the hope of progressing into a more active position in the theatre. Lucy, what could that be?'

'Assistant stage manager,' said Lucy confidently. 'It's what you might call the first rung on the ladder for someone who wants a life in the theatre. Many currently successful actors and actresses began in that way, and we may even find a part for Esther in the upcoming play. Not Ophelia, obviously, but there are several walk-on parts as Ladies of the Court of Elsinore. She could perhaps aspire to play one of those.'

'While she's at it,' Percy suggested, 'she might start making a noise about how Shakespeare never wrote enough parts for women, and that this reflects a general attitude towards women in general.'

'You're forgetting Lady Macbeth, and Desdemona for that matter,' Lucy pointed out. 'Shakespeare's characters reflected the history of the age that he was seeking to depict, that was all. Modern writers tend to depict women as governesses and companions, because that's the role they occupy in contemporary society.'

'Which will give Esther even more reason to begin sounding off about how this state of affairs still prevails,' Percy suggested, 'enough to motivate Simon Abelman's interest in getting Esther to meet his lady friend, Florence Bannister.'

'He might get interested in Esther herself, instead,' Jack said unhappily.

'I'm a respectable married lady with children, remember?' Esther reassured him. 'And why would he be likely to find me attractive?'

'You're Jewish, disarmingly beautiful for your age, and you share his political views, that's why,' Jack replied.

Percy nodded. 'You've just given me another idea, Jack.'

'Well, don't give it to Esther,' Jack insisted, but there was no stopping Percy.

'If Abelman finds himself attracted to Esther, so much the better. We're trying to get him to let down his guard, remember — to find out to what extent he's prepared to side with this WSPU lot. The more he's encouraged to share confidences with her, the more likely he is to reveal that.'

'I've suddenly gone off the whole idea,' Jack muttered, but Esther dug him in the ribs.

'And I've suddenly warmed to it even more,' she said. 'I have no objection to being lavished with attention by a gallant young actor, and I may say that I'm getting a lovely warm feeling, just watching Jack getting jealous.'

'I'm *not* getting jealous,' Jack insisted, 'just concerned in case our carefully laid plans go awry.'

'They won't if you both stick closely to the plans we've agreed on,' Percy assured them all, 'and the sooner we set about those, the faster we can prove Lucy's innocence. And before anyone asks, I'll be taking my first actions tomorrow.'

If those who'd installed the door locks on the second-floor apartments of the splendid late Georgian building in Green Street, just north of Mayfair's Grosvenor Square, thought that they were resistant to the selection of tools possessed by Percy Enright, then they were mistaken.

He was inside the front hall of the apartment in seconds, and noted that a cloying perfumed aroma still lingered there. Making a mental note to ask Lucy if Valentine Primrose had been in the habit of dousing himself in lavender, Percy progressed down an ornate hall with alabaster busts of famous actors, each mounted on a white podium and bearing the name of the subject on a brass plaque, until he came to what must have been intended to be a kitchen, but which looked more like the interior of a Greek mausoleum with its white-panelled cupboards. It was in immaculate condition, creating the impression that no cooking ever took place here, and likewise the three bathrooms that ran off to one side gave no indication that anyone had ever bathed, shaved, or performed bodily functions within them.

There were two bedrooms, each with an adjoining dressing room. Percy entered the larger of the two and opened the wardrobe carefully, his hands protected by ladies' gloves that he always carried for clandestine visits to other people's houses while they were absent. He found the usual fashionable gentleman's attire — suits, shoes, socks and underwear, all bearing the trademarks of fashionable West End outfitters. But there were striking differences when it came to the second bedroom, which like the first was graced with a wall-length wardrobe.

The clothing in this second wardrobe was of a different quality. It was smart, and in good condition — the sort of clothing that might be worn by a bank clerk, a schoolteacher or an insurance salesman, but it did not have the high-society quality of the garments hanging in the wardrobe in the first bedroom, nor did it appear to fit a man of the same size. There also did not appear to be enough of it to constitute a full complement of clothing for a man who lived here, and it was Percy's first instinct that whoever had occupied this bedroom had done so as a regular guest, but not a permanent resident.

Having completed his provisional survey of Primrose's former residence, Percy was in the process of letting himself back out into the hallway and restoring the front door to its original locked and closed position when he froze at the sound of a woman's challenge.

'Are you another of Mr Primrose's former friends?' she asked.

Percy turned to address her as he quickly dreamed up a reason for letting himself out of Primrose's former apartment. 'No,' he replied, 'I'm from the Crown Property Agency in Marylebone, and I was assessing this apartment for possible purchase from Mr Primrose's estate. However, I noticed that someone else has been living here recently. Do you know where I might contact him?'

'You could always leave him a note to contact you,' the lady replied as she eyed him suspiciously. 'And in any case, that apartment is rented from the same agency as mine, so you'd need to speak to them about purchasing it, since Mr Primrose didn't own it as such. Nor did the other gentleman who frequently stayed there.'

'It might help if you could give me his name,' Percy ventured.

The lady frowned. 'You must surely know it, if you're who you say you are. Or are you a burglar?'

'Do I look like a burglar?'

'I've no idea what burglars look like, but you *do* you look a little shifty, if you'll pardon me for saying so. Perhaps I should go back inside my own apartment and make a telephone call to the police.'

'And finish up looking foolish?' Percy challenged her. 'I can assure you that I'm genuine, and there really is no reason for you to call the police. I'm leaving now anyway, and as you can see, I have nothing in my possession, so clearly I haven't been stealing anything.'

'All the same,' the woman replied as she backed away towards her own front door, 'I shall telephone the Regency Agency and let them know that a somewhat dubious character was inspecting their property. They're only a few streets away and can have someone round here in a very short time, so I suggest that you make yourself scarce without delay.'

'Interfering old sow!' Percy muttered to himself as he descended the ornate staircase and made his way back towards the bustling street. 'But at least she gave me something valuable to work on, even if she didn't intend to. Let's hope that "a few streets away" was literally true.' Then he blushed and hurried on when he saw passers-by looking pityingly at him as he talked to himself.

Five streets away he found Regency Properties, located between a high-price flower shop and an optician's display window. He pushed his way through the heavy glass door, causing a bell to tinkle in warning as he made his way across a plush carpet towards a mahogany desk, behind which sat a formidable-looking lady wearing the sort of spectacles that appeared to possess wings.

'My name's Percival, and I'm from Crown Properties,' he announced as he extracted a card from his wallet and held it high in the air, and far enough away for the lady not to be able to read its contents. It was, in fact, an entry permit into the royal enclosure at the Royal Horticultural Society Great Spring Show of 1887, in which Percy's roses had been a prize-winner. He had kept it because of the impressive royal crest that was displayed at the top, which at a cursory glance could be passed off as confirmation of his employment at whatever organisation he had just invented.

'We're not currently seeking new employees,' the lady replied haughtily.

Percy gave her a withering look. 'Which is perhaps as well, since I'm not in need of a new employer. What I *am* seeking to ascertain is whether or not Apartment Two in Addlebrook Mansions in Green Street is likely to be coming up for sale following the unfortunate recent death of Mr Primrose.'

'That would be one of the rentals that we manage, presumably?'

'So I was told by the lady residing in Number One, who will no doubt be telephoning shortly to advise you of my interest. I have a client who is most desirous of acquiring the property, if a suitable price can be negotiated.'

The lady rose from her chair and walked around the front of the counter in order to open the top drawer of a filing cabinet down one wall and extract a file, which she took back to her desk and opened. After consulting its contents, she looked back up at Percy, shaking her head.

'The property isn't actually yet in vacant possession. We received instructions from the lawyer for the executor of the late Mr Primrose's estate, to the effect that a gentleman who was residing there on an occasional basis is to be allowed to remain until further instructed.'

'And the name of this gentleman?' Percy asked hopefully.

The lady's mouth set like a rabbit trap. 'That information is of course confidential.'

'Even to a potential purchaser?'

'*Especially* to a potential purchaser represented by a rival agency. Good morning, Mr Percival.'

She looked back down at the papers she'd been studying when Percy had entered the office, and he recognised a brick wall when he saw one. But, as he was fond of advising those with less experience than himself, there was more than one way to skin a cat.

Back at home, Percy made an urgent telephone call to Jack. 'Are you still on the routine circulation list of the previous day's crimes?' he asked.

'Of course,' Jack confirmed, 'but why do you ask, and what do you want to know?'

'Nothing yet,' Percy replied, 'but for the next few mornings, please look out for a report of a burglary at Apartment Two, Addlebrook Mansions in Green Street, Mayfair. I want to know the identity of the person who reports it.'

'How do you know in advance that there's going to be a burglary there, or can I guess?'

'Probably. But for the avoidance of doubt, be advised that your old Uncle Percy's about to effect a felonious entrance to a prestigious address in the "high society" end of town.'

He grinned to himself as he put down the phone. All he needed to do now was await nightfall.

CHAPTER SIX

In truth, Jack had enough to worry about, without acting as Percy's spy inside Scotland Yard. Apart from his commitment to pose as a hopeful actor, he had his own restless children to manage, as well as worrying about how Esther would react to some pretentious barrister called Simon Abelman when she set about attracting his attention.

First and foremost among the several issues threatening to turn his brain into mashed potato was his thirteen-year-old son Bertie's return to the "chocolate soldier" organisation established some years ago by his near neighbour the Earl of Essex, who owned Cassiobury Park, almost two hundred acres of verdant parkland that adjoined Jack's home, and began just over his rear fence. The park had become a popular recreational attraction for local Watford residents, and the earl who owned it was very generous in allowing them to walk, exercise, play ball, ride horses, and generally enjoy the open space.

He also had a hankering to be the local "warrior gentleman hero", and was a Major in the Volunteer Brigade of the Hertfordshire Regiment, into which he was untiring in his efforts to recruit volunteers. Some years ago he'd hit upon the idea of recruiting boys as young as seven into what he called a Boys' Battalion, and Bertie, given his lifelong obsession with toy soldiers and anything military in nature, had persuaded Jack to allow him to join, despite Jack's gloomy prediction that this seemingly harmless outlet for youthful energy would prove to be a recruiting source for men to be sent off to pointless wars.

Three years ago Jack had taken the opportunity to prevent his own son being sucked into this fate when Bertie had sprained his ankle in a badly supervised, and totally unnecessary, attempt to scale a wall using only a rope. Jack had insisted that Bertie was to attend no more gatherings of what he had called "that ramshackle boys' outfit." But Bertie's enthusiasm for military matters, far from diminishing as the result of this withdrawal, had only intensified, together with a resentment that had threatened to estrange father and son.

Then came the day when a very nervous Alice had announced the arrival of the Earl of Essex in person at Jack and Esther's house. It was a Saturday, and Jack was at home, having just finished breakfast with Esther. When Alice told them that she'd installed the earl in the sitting room, they made their way there in some trepidation, wondering if, during their regular romps in the park, Bertie and Annabelle had been guilty of some bad behaviour.

The earl rose to meet them with a broad smile and held out his hand for Jack to shake. 'I don't believe we've actually met in person,' he said, beaming, 'but my thanks for being such a good neighbour, and of course I heard complimentary things about your good work in the Metropolitan Police from your son, during our all-too-brief acquaintance. And I'm here in connection with him, as it transpires.'

'I do hope he and his adopted sister haven't been up to any mischief,' Jack muttered, but the earl's smile didn't diminish.

'Not at all, and please hear me out. I'd like you to reconsider your decision to withdraw Bertie from my Boys' Battalion. He was one of the most promising, enthusiastic and lively of those who I originally recruited, and he has officer potential.'

'As an officer of *what*, precisely?' Jack asked as his hackles threatened to rise.

'The Hertfordshire Regiment, of course,' the earl reminded him. 'A fine volunteer force that will one day be part of our nation's defence against any foreign threat.'

'And get the men in it killed in the process,' Jack replied, glaring back at him.

'Of course, there are always casualties in war,' the earl conceded, 'but it may not come to that. And there can be no finer career for a man than in a disciplined body of men taking orders from superior and well-trained officers. You'll appreciate that for yourself, of course, since there are many valid comparisons between an army regiment and a police force.'

'The answer's no,' Jack insisted.

Esther placed a restraining hand on his arm as she joined the conversation. 'My brother was — and still is — an army officer,' she told the earl, 'and it certainly made a fine man out of him. He also confided in me, during a conversation when we were briefly reunited during a period of his leave, that one is less likely to die in combat if one is an officer than if one is among the general body of fighting infantry. Is that the case?'

'Statistically it most certainly is,' the earl confirmed, 'although, of course, to maintain high morale among the men, that fact is not generally bandied about.'

'And how real is the prospect that England will soon go to war with another country, perhaps Germany?' she persisted.

The earl frowned slightly, then inclined his head when answering her. 'I am obviously not privy to current intelligence from the War Office, although as an officer of a reserve battalion I am regularly told of any need to consider mobilisation of troops to "standby" status. So far as I am aware, there is no immediate prospect of men being required to depart overseas, or of any impending threat to the sanctity of our shores. However, it seems that Germany is amassing recruits, and we are obliged to do likewise.'

'All the more reason to keep Bertie out of it,' Jack muttered, but Esther wasn't finished.

'If and when a war is declared, you rely on young men volunteering, don't you?'

'Indeed,' the earl confirmed.

'How old do they need to be before they will be accepted?'

'If they're medically fit, they can lawfully volunteer at fourteen, for non-combat roles such as drummers, messengers and the like. For fighting, they need to be seventeen.'

'And once they've signed the papers, not even their parents can retrieve them?'

'No, and if they change their minds and desert — well, it would not be good for them to do that.'

'These youngsters of fourteen, in what you called "non-combat" roles, what's their survival rate?'

'Very low,' the earl replied as he suddenly appreciated her ploy. 'The enemy make short work of young boys caught out in the open, beating the drum at the side of the front row of men on the march, or scurrying from one hidey-hole to another with messages.'

Esther turned to Jack with tears in her eyes. 'Bertie will be fourteen next year, and all that's filled his mind since he could walk is soldiers, the army and battle tactics. If he were to slip away in defiance of what you try to impose on him, he'd be lost to us, and with an enhanced prospect of getting killed. On the other hand, as an officer in his early twenties, or whatever age, he'd have the same chances of survival as my brother Abe. Which is it to be, Jack?'

Jack argued, swore, and even blasphemed, but Esther had won the day. The following week Bertie found himself back in the Brigade, this time proudly sporting the short-trousered khaki uniform with which he'd been supplied, with a corporal's stripes on his short-sleeved shirt.

There had also been difficulties with the remaining children when they learned that Jack and Esther were about to join Aunt Lucy's theatre group. Their oldest child, Lily, only days away from her fifteenth birthday, had become an expert seamstress under her mother's guidance, and when she overheard a conversation between Esther and Aunt Lucy regarding various theatrical costumes that were in urgent need of repair, she'd campaigned, without success, to be allowed to go with Esther to the theatre and find a more challenging outlet for her needlework than dolls' clothes and running repairs on her own school smock. She was now sulking permanently. It didn't help that she and Annabelle had now taken their places in the recently enlarged Senior Class at Cassiobury House School, which was taught by the school's proprietor and headmistress Emily Allsop, who constantly reported back to Esther that the girls seemed determined to resist education of any description.

Annabelle was also displaying the same resentment at being excluded from the theatre, where she imagined that she could write plays to be performed by its actors. Her love of writing stories had transcended into something more ambitious, and her exposure to the works of Shakespeare, Congreve and Sheridan had opened up another potential field of aspiration for her literary endeavours. The atmosphere at home, with the two girls sighing and flouncing, was rapidly becoming unbearable.

The natural alliance between Annabelle, Lily and Bertie had effectively cut the family in half, with ten-year-old Miriam and nine-year-old Thomas left in a sort of isolation in which they giggled, plotted, and demonstrated their ingenuity for practical jokes designed to attract their parents' attention. And in the middle of all this domestic upheaval, Jack was struggling to become an actor.

Lucy had posted him a copy of the text of *Hamlet*, and he'd eagerly read those parts of it in which the fiery Laertes establishes his personality, and dominates many of the key events that lead to the tragic death of himself and the hero. Realising that she herself would also be called upon to simulate theatrical ambition, Esther had taken to listening to Jack extolling lines from various parts of the play, and as tactfully as possible she had helped him make his delivery more credible. But at the end of the day, as an actor he made a very good chief inspector of police.

Several days after the telephone call from Percy regarding a possible burglary in the offing, Jack was able to confirm that it had taken place, not that Percy seemed surprised to hear of it.

'The report speaks of the forcing of the front door with a crude implement of some sort, and the complete emptying of a wardrobe of men's clothing from one of the bedrooms,' Jack told him. 'There's also a statement from a lady living in a neighbouring apartment, who claims to have seen what she describes as "a shabby little man" behaving suspiciously at the door of the apartment a few days prior to that. Do you include "shabby" in your extensive repertoire?'

'Dispense with the jokes, and tell me who made the complaint,' Percy insisted eagerly.

'Strangely enough, a man called Leopold Carter, who claims to have been living there,' Jack said with satisfaction. 'You would seem to have flushed out something important, if that name rings the correct bell in my memory.'

'It does indeed,' Percy confirmed, 'and it adds a new dimension to the personal connections between the actors when Primrose was killed. Clearly he had an ongoing relationship with Leo Carter. No wonder the poor man was so devastated when his was the hand that killed his boyfriend. The question now arises as to whether or not someone planned it that way, as a final irony.'

'Perhaps it was just a straightforward lovers' tiff,' Jack suggested.

'If that were the case, why did Carter carry out the deed so publicly, and in circumstances that might point the finger at him? Why not just do him in at home, then make it look like an accident, or perhaps transport the body to somewhere else to be found? No, the answer is far more subtle than that. If anything, the revelation of the private relationship between Carter and the deceased has just muddied the waters even more.'

'If you say so,' Jack conceded, 'which of course makes it even more important for Esther and me to get inside that theatre group with our eyes and ears open.'

'And how are matters progressing in that regard?'

'Very poorly, in my case,' Jack admitted. 'She tries not to show it, but Esther's clearly not impressed with my ability as an actor. How on earth I'll get past the audition I've no idea. It's only a matter of days until those auditions, and I think I've found yet another way to make a fool of myself.'

'Courage, Jack,' Percy urged him. 'Courage and an undying self-belief. I've spent years pretending to be different people, and if you convince yourself that you really *are* that person, you can usually get away with it.'

'If you say so,' Jack replied, unconvinced. 'But what's your next move, now that you've exposed the real relationship between Carter and Primrose, and for all intents and purposes eliminated Carter?'

'I move on to the next candidate from the remaining four,' Percy told him. 'Starting with Graves, who's one of those that a certain Government department wishes me to investigate. They gave me a good deal of background from their own original recruitment files, and I'm off to his old school, posing as a Special Branch investigator in the hope that Ernest Graves is revealed as another possible "special friend" of the dear departed.'

'Good luck with that,' Jack said with a chuckle. 'What, if anything, do you want me to do in the meantime?'

'Learn your lines, and try to look and sound like an actor in the making. Somehow I think that my task will prove to be the easier of the two.'

'This is highly unusual,' complained Herbert Manning, Deputy Headmaster of Kilburn Grammar School. 'I've never been asked for this sort of information before, and I'm not sure that I'm authorised to provide you with it. But in the absence of the headmaster, who's confined to his bed with what is believed to be a bad case of scarlet fever, I have to make the decisions. You *did* assure me that it's in the nation's interests?'

'That's perhaps putting it a little dramatically,' Percy replied in his assumed role of Thomas Percival, Senior Recruitment Officer, Intelligence Branch of the War Office. 'But you'll appreciate that before we can consider anyone for a more senior role in such a sensitive area of government as Naval Intelligence, we have to be absolutely certain that there is nothing in a man's background that might make him a security risk. And, I should perhaps emphasise, the process is entirely informal. Not even your headmaster needs to know that we've had this little conversation.'

'That's a comfort of sorts,' said Manning, the relief obvious in his face. 'You'll appreciate that in the days when Ernest Graves passed through the school, I was only a House Master, and he wasn't even in my house. But I remember him well enough, given his outstanding performances in Mathematics, which is one of the subjects I teach. Mathematics and Rugby Football.'

'He obviously put his analytical skills to good use, as a cipher clerk,' Percy observed. 'But what do you remember about the boy himself?'

'A bit of a show-off, as I remember him,' Manning replied. 'He was always the first to volunteer to take part in our school dramatic productions, which in those days tended to be Shakespearean in nature, and not all boys are fond of Shakespeare. I half expected that he'd become an actor when he left school, and if you tell me that he's now closeted away in some Government office doing routine clerical work, well, I'm surprised to hear it. Because he was so confident, so — well, so *dominant*, I think would be the correct term. He always had a group of admirers around him. You know — other boys who wanted to bask in his light. Sometimes he'd make use of that to create unrest among them, seeding arguments, then standing back and enjoying the resulting confrontations.'

'Any specific incidents you can recall?' Percy asked.

'There was *one* such incident that I recall personally,' Manning reminisced, 'since one of my several responsibilities in those days was the supervision of our tuck shop. The woman who ran it for us was a local minister's wife, and she would bring her daughter along to assist on some occasions. The young lady was about fifteen years old and strikingly attractive, and inevitably the more senior boys would vie for her attention. Anyway, Graves persuaded one boy — Mitchell, I think his name was — that another boy called Andrews had been walking out with her, and the two came to blows. When it all came out that Andrews hadn't been seeing the girl at all, and that Graves had been the one to suggest he had, Graves just smirked and said something along the lines of, "People are so easily manipulated, and it was so easy that it wasn't even a challenge." He was punished for that by being set extra Maths homework a little above his educational level, and he completed it in an astonishingly short time. So, a bit of an enigma — hugely talented, a born leader of men, but inclined to be mischievous. Does that assist in your decision as to whether or not he's suitable for a promotion?'

'Indeed it does, Mr Manning,' Percy replied, 'and I shall make valuable use of what you've told me. Once again, rest assured that no-one will learn of this conversation.'

When Percy got home, he put in another call to Jack.

'Watch out carefully for Graves,' he warned him, 'and guard your back. The man's a devious serpent who enjoys playing one person off against another. Once you're established in the Holborn Players, I want you to look for evidence that he employed that particular talent to bring about the death of Primrose.'

CHAPTER SEVEN

Esther needed the protracted illness of Headmistress Emily Allsop like a hole in the head at this moment, but she owed her so much. It had been Emily who'd recognised Esther's natural talent as a teacher when she'd enrolled her on the training course in East Ham over eight years ago, after which she had invited to join her as her Deputy Headmistress when she'd taken over as the proprietor of Cassiobury House Private School. Esther had never looked back and had been able to enrol two of her own children — Lily, then Miriam — into her combined Primary One and Two classes, in which Annabelle had already been a pupil.

Now dear Emily was confined to bed with a racking cough and a weakness in her limbs that rendered her incapable of teaching her own Senior Class, the first of its kind to be established at Cassiobury House, and crucial to the school's ongoing financial security. It was the least that Esther could do to combine duties, setting exercises for one class to conduct in silence, but unsupervised, while she gave her attention to the other.

It was an additional distraction that she could do without, given her impending entry into Lucy's theatre group under an assumed name, but loyalty was something that Esther had never lacked. And her loyalty to Jack, the worst actor she could imagine, would place additional strain on her, but he was someone else to whom she owed everything.

The dreaded day had come. It was Saturday morning, and the crucial meeting of the Holborn Players was scheduled for ten o'clock, during which the roles for the planned production of *Hamlet* would be decided. Jack felt as if he was walking to his own execution as he strolled down St Albans Road on his way to the station, where he'd take the eighty-twenty train to Euston and transfer from there to Holborn by omnibus.

There was a chance that the omnibus he caught would be one of the new red ones that were powered by what they called internal combustion engines, but they rattled even more than the horse-drawn ones, and the fumes that they generated were said to be harmful to health. Perhaps in the near future he'd have the option of travelling underground on one of those trains that bustled many feet below pavement level, but somehow the idea of burrowing under the earth in a smoky open carriage didn't appeal to him. He was happy to settle for an older omnibus, horse-drawn, while he prepared himself for his ordeal.

He didn't even have Esther for company, because in order to maintain the pretence it had been agreed that he and Esther would not arrive together. Instead, Esther had spent the previous night at Lucy and Teddy's home in Southampton Place, above Teddy's architectural practice offices, and she and Lucy were the first to arrive at the theatre. As the members of the company drifted in ahead of the ten o'clock meeting, several of them cast curious glances at the smart, attractive but nervous-looking lady in her early forties who seemed reluctant to leave Lucy's side as the two of them organised the chairs in the main room that doubled as a 'dressing room'.

Lucy then gave Esther a brief tour of the remaining rooms that the theatre group rented, including the kitchen, finishing with the theatre itself, with its one hundred and fifty chairs and wide stage, hidden behind heavy red drapes that Lucy showed Esther how to operate as part of her assumed future duties.

'We can normally rely on having a stage hand to operate this heavy winch,' Lucy puffed as she heaved on its handle, causing the curtains to swish open slowly, 'but there are occasions when "needs must", and you have to get the hang of this pulley. Don't try and turn it all in one go, with the one hand — it works better if you do it this way, hand over hand.'

'Good to see the ladies getting down to men's work,' came an imperious voice from the wings, 'but if either of you is pregnant, the strain on the stomach muscles can cause a miscarriage.'

'Meet Dr Henry Gloucester,' Lucy said. 'It's good to see you here ahead of time, Henry, since I'd like you to meet my sister-in-law, who'll be joining us as an assistant stage manager. Please make her feel welcome.'

'I'd be delighted to do so,' Henry said with a leer, 'since ladies are my speciality.'

Lucy turned Esther with a grin. 'He's impossibly forward with every lady he meets, and I sometimes wonder how his patients react.'

'Every meeting with me is a treat for a lady,' said Henry, 'but where are the others, and have you settled on a part for me?'

'Fittingly, I've got you provisionally marked down to play Claudius, the wicked uncle,' Lucy told him. 'And since I'll probably be playing Gertrude, this will mean that you and I were conducting an illicit affair before you murdered Hamlet's father and became my husband.'

'There have to be *some* perks in this hazardous theatrical ocean that we all sail, dear lady,' Henry replied smoothly, 'and may I assume that when looking for a Thespian lover, you naturally thought of me?'

'Settle down, Henry, and go and wait with the others in the dressing room,' Lucy chided him, 'while I show Esther where the remaining facilities are hidden away. We might try the catwalk next, so be gone with you.'

By the time that Lucy and Esther returned to the main room, most of the other members of the theatre group had drifted in, including an apprehensive-looking Jack. Lucy clapped her hands in order to get their attention, then made the introductions.

'At a time when our gallant group of players is facing the challenge of falling numbers, it's a considerable pleasure to be able to welcome two new members to our fold. The first is this delightful lady alongside me, who I'm proud to acknowledge as my sister-in-law, Esther Masefield, married to my husband's brother, Charles. Esther is gifted with needle and thread, and has considerable experience as a wardrobe mistress in various provincial theatres located in towns to which her husband's business interests have taken them over the years. She's developed a hankering for taking to the boards herself, and is therefore joining us as a second assistant stage manager.'

'She can make the next lot of bloody sandwiches, then,' muttered a somewhat dowdy young woman seated to the rear of the assembled company. 'The last lot I made went to waste.'

'I think we all know how that came about, Alice,' Lucy replied consolingly. 'Were it not for the tragic death of poor old Val, I'm sure we would all have been enjoying them after the final performance in that run.'

'I'm just warning the newcomer that being an assistant stage manager doesn't guarantee you a speaking part,' Alice replied grumpily. 'I should know — I've been doing it for the best part of two years.'

Esther smiled back uncertainly, making a mental note that this woman, whoever she was, had been there on *the* night, and might be able to add something valuable to their knowledge of what had taken place backstage. Then her attention was drawn back to Lucy, as she introduced Jack to the company.

'We have another new member to welcome, so please stand up, Jack.'

Jack rose to his feet, hoping that his shaking knees weren't visible through his fashionable trousers that went with his fashionable jacket, both of which he hoped made him look like a successful insurance entrepreneur.

'I have to thank my husband for finding Jack,' Lucy enthused. 'He's an insurance broker, and Teddy consulted him regarding a new development in Harrow. He came to dinner, and during our general conversation it emerged that he has for many years dreamed of exploring an interest in amateur dramatics that he first developed during his school days. He strikes me as having great potential as a portrayer of mature men who still retain some of their youthful fire and vigour, which in terms of *Hamlet* of course means Laertes. He's already given me a few readings for the part, and I've asked him to come along to today's auditions to perhaps finalise his role. I have no doubt that others among you might be aspiring to play that role, but of course there's no shortage of other possibilities, given the preponderance of male parts in the work.'

'More's the pity,' Esther muttered loudly enough to be hard by the others, and was aware of a haughty-looking young man a few seats away giving her a searching look.

'Indeed,' Lucy agreed, 'but it's as well that we aren't called upon to find more women for our upcoming production, given our imbalance in members. I shall almost certainly have to assume the role of Queen Gertrude, since even with heavy make-up I'd be manifestly absurd as Ophelia. Fortunately, my long-term association with our good friends the Chelsea

Players, about which I hear occasional grumbles from you, has stood us in great stead, and I have high hopes that a young lady called Constance Hartley will agree to give us the benefit of her simulated madness. And so, let's progress to the stage, shall we, and see how matters fall out?'

Jack sat dumbly in the second row of the audience seats while Lucy invited her leading actors, one by one, to mount the stage and read for those parts she believed they would best suit. Henry Gloucester was rapidly confirmed as King Claudius, which part he appeared to be able to deliver with his own naturally oily charm, combined with a suggestion of underlying evil. Arthur Dennistoun, inclined to be something of a scene-stealer, was easily persuaded to take the role of the gravedigger when assured that he could play it for all the laughs he could get.

The tension in the air was palpable when it came to casting Hamlet himself, and both Simon Abelman and Ernest Graves put up good portrayals of a less than young man haunted by self-doubt and indecision. In the end Lucy tactfully chose Simon for the lead role, easing the way for Jack to be cast as Laertes, and Ernest was consoled with the part of Polonius, the father of both Laertes and Ophelia.

Finally it was Jack's turn, and as he climbed onto the stage, trying not to shake with the fear of making a complete ass of himself, he remembered the advice that Percy had given him: to actually make yourself believe that you're the person you're pretending to be. He therefore listened carefully when Lucy asked him to open the script at the point in Act 3, Scene 5, when Laertes, having returned to Elsinore to learn of the death of his father, is suddenly confronted with Ophelia's obvious madness.

'Remember,' Lucy urged him, 'she's the person you most love in the world, and she's suddenly lost to you. You were already in a heightened emotional state regarding the death of your father, and now this comes as a double blow.'

Jack took a deep breath and held up the script as he imagined Ophelia to be Esther. How would he feel if she were still there in body, but he'd lost her companionship, buried inside a brain that was no longer hers to control?

The lump was already in his throat before he even began, and his voice cracked several times as he delivered the lines:

'By heaven, thy madness shall be paid with weight
Till our scale turn the beam! O rose of May,
Dear maid, kind sister, sweet Ophelia!
O heavens, is't possible a young maid's wits
Should be as mortal as an old man's life?'

By the time he'd finished there were tears rolling down his cheeks, and Lucy was staring at him, open-mouthed. Esther was reaching urgently into the sleeve of her gown for her kerchief, and from the remainder of the cast came murmurs of appreciation, and a quiet clap from Leopold, who added, 'Bravo, young man.'

'I think we'd all benefit from a pot of tea,' Lucy finally suggested, and Alice Bennett volunteered to make it. Esther offered to assist, and as she put the pot on to boil, and Alice began laying out the cups and saucers on a tray, the opportunity presented itself to learn something that might be of assistance to Percy.

'I hope you aren't going to resent me joining the group,' Esther said in her smallest voice. 'Only, from what you said earlier it sounded as if you really hoped to become an actress, but were reduced to making sandwiches.'

'Of course I won't resent you,' Alice assured her, 'because you're no different from me. If there's someone else to do the mundane tasks that have been assigned to me over the past two years, then perhaps I'll finally get to walk on stage and actually deliver a line, rather than just standing there like some sort of shop window mannequin. Presumably Lucy promised you a walk-on role as a lady of the Court, providing some sort of backdrop to the male actors?'

'Yes, she did, as a matter of fact,' Esther replied, 'and from what you tell me, that's about as far as I'll progress towards becoming an actress.'

'Just don't build up your hopes, that's all I'm saying,' Alice warned. 'The water's coming up to the boil, so pass me the tea urn, would you? It's over on the far side there.'

'Let's hope they appreciate this tea more than they did your sandwiches,' Esther observed sympathetically as the hot water hit the tea urn.

Alice shrugged. 'They didn't deliberately reject them. It was because one of our actors was accidently killed when one of the daggers malfunctioned. It was a terrible business, and all the actors were sent home in a state of shock. The sandwiches were intended for a celebration party at the end of the final performance, but of course, as events transpired, that never took place.'

'It must have been awful to watch,' Esther sympathised.

Alice shook her head. 'I didn't actually see it, although I heard the commotion. Then all these bobbies arrived and took over, and Lucy sent me home.'

'Did the police take a statement from you?'

'Eventually, although I had to go to the police station in Grays Inn Road to give it. I'd been too busy laying out the sandwiches and lemonade, after the table was finally free of all the props. I'd waited long enough to do that, skulking in the kitchen while all the male actors argued over whose knife was whose.'

'Weren't they all the same?'

'They certainly looked it,' Alice replied, 'which is why I was so surprised when I heard them arguing about it. And of course, in the end, one of them misfired, as it were, and poor old Val — Valentine Primrose, he was the one playing Caesar — was fatally stabbed.'

'Typical men,' Esther snorted, 'arguing over which of them gets the best toy. I've got two boys at home who can create a war over who gets to ride the rocking horse.'

'Well, the ones here behave just like that, you'll find,' Alice warned her. 'I was very surprised when Simon — Simon Abelman — didn't object to that good-looking newcomer getting the part he'd been hankering after.'

'But he's playing Hamlet,' Esther reminded her, 'so presumably he's more than consoled with that.'

'You're probably right,' Alice agreed, 'but he's just typical of the childish male behaviour that we see around here. There seems to be something about men who want to be actors that makes them sensitive to what they perceive to be slights, and quick to argue about who gets which part. Or, that night, which knife.'

'If all the knives were the same, what did it matter?' Esther mused.

Alice nodded. 'Precisely. I was back here in the kitchen, so I only heard their carry-on. I was waiting until the table in the changing room was empty of props, so that I could carry in the sandwiches and lemonade, and two of them — or it might have been three — were arguing over who was to get which knife. I'm pretty sure that Leo Carter was one of them, since his voice is higher than the other two. Leo made the same point that you just made — what did it matter? — but someone else, who could have been Simon or Ernie, was insisting that Leo take the knife that was left, since he — Simon or Ernie, like I said — was insisting on taking the one he'd already picked up, and was about to go on stage with. It was all a bit pointless, really, since when I was finally able to go in there and lay the refreshments on the table, there was one knife left on it, which I put back in the props cupboard. Imagine, five grown men arguing over who gets which of five identical knives, when there are six of them available anyway! Now, let's get this tea in there, shall we? You take the teapot, and I'll carry in the cups and saucers on a tray. Then I'll come back for the milk and sugar.'

While Alice had been giving Esther vital new information without realising it, Jack had been surrounded by the remaining male actors as they sat on chairs around the table in the dressing room, on which they were anticipating the delivery of tea. They were congratulating him on his performance, and Ernest in particular was fulsome in his praise as he sat next to Jack and placed a warm hand on his arm. Jack felt curiously repelled by the man's touch, but smiled through gritted teeth as he confessed, 'I really don't know what came over me. I just tried to imagine how I'd feel if it were my wife, and it just sort of came out.'

'A born actor!' Ernest insisted. 'That's how I do it — imagining myself in the part. Now, thanks to Lucy's insistence I shall have to try to imagine myself as an old man. It won't come easy, since I have so much youthful vigour still in me, if you get what I mean. At least you got to play Hamlet, Simon,' he called across to his rival. 'That should satisfy your ego for the next few months.'

'No more than I merit,' Simon replied coldly, 'and when I need to imagine what self-doubt feels like, I might model myself on Leo over there.'

Clearly there was no love lost between Simon and Leopold, Jack concluded, and Ernest was clearly someone who enjoyed causing trouble, then walking away, just as Percy had discovered. He was just thinking that it might be appropriate to arrange another Sunday lunch meeting for them all when Lucy took the vacant chair on the other side and told him, 'You clearly have a natural ability that I shall enjoy developing. We rehearse on Tuesday and Thursday evenings, and, I'm afraid, the whole of Saturday as well. Will that be convenient for you? We'll be starting with Act One, which only involves you a little, so even if you arrive late, we should be able to accommodate you without disrupting the rehearsal.'

'That's very kind of you,' Jack replied, just as Alice and Esther appeared with the tea.

'Presumably you resent having to serve us tea, rather than joining us in a discussion of the male parts that we'll be embracing for the foreseeable future?' Simon called across to Esther.

'I don't mind making tea,' Esther replied coolly, 'since it's what women do, and I'd hate to drink a cup of tea made by a man. But it's high time that you men realised that we women can do more than make tea.'

'Believe me, I do, thanks to my lady friend, Flo,' Simon said with a smile. 'You should meet her some time — she often pops in to join me after rehearsals have finished on weeknights, then sometimes we go for a late supper at a little restaurant we favour in Old Compton Street. It's owned and run entirely by women, and they specialise in home cooking, not all that French rubbish that male chefs seem to delight in making.'

'I'll look forward to that,' Esther said, looking more cheerful. 'Now, let me revert to the role that society seems to have imposed on me and pour you a cup of tea. Do you like the milk in first, or afterwards?'

As the morning drifted into early afternoon, Lucy announced that they'd done enough for the day. 'I thought that for once we might enjoy a Saturday afternoon off. Once we get fully into rehearsals there'll be no letting up, I'm afraid.'

'What about the remaining roles?' Arthur asked. 'Do you want me to double up in another role, aside from that of the gravedigger?'

'Almost certainly Fortinbras, who's the Prince of Norway, and whose scenes don't clash with the gravedigger's. There shouldn't be a need for any hasty costume changes. As for the rest, I suspect that we'll be raiding the Cambridge Players again, since we don't have enough males of our own, more's the pity. But if nothing else we made a great find with young Jack here, and I look forward to working more closely with him.'

'So do I,' Ernest murmured, sending a shiver up Jack's spine.

The actors headed off one by one, leaving only Jack, Lucy, Esther and Alice. An awkward silence fell as each of the Enrights tried to think of some way of leaving together without alerting suspicion. Then Alice asked, 'Jack — I may call you Jack, I assume? — would you have any objection to walking me to the omnibus stop at the bottom of Endell Street? I live in Blackfriars, and there's a convenient service that runs from there.'

'I'd be more than happy to do so,' Jack replied graciously, 'although I live in the other direction, so I'll need to double back afterwards. However, it's no hardship to be escorting a charming young lady like yourself, and I can come back past here on my way to High Holborn.'

Hoping that Lucy and Esther had taken the hint, Jack did as requested. He listened to Alice's incessant chatter about her frustrations over not getting acting parts before waving her onto her omnibus, then doubling back to Endell Street, where Lucy and Esther were waiting for him on the pavement outside the theatre.

'How did you fare with the "charming young lady"?' Esther asked tartly.

Jack grinned. 'I think she has an eye for me, which may come in useful in the future.'

'Then you won't complain if that charming Simon Abelman shows me some attention?' Esther asked.

'How did you both get on?' Lucy cut in. 'And genuine congratulations on your acting ability, Jack. You were astounding. I had no idea that my big brother was so talented.'

'I'm anxious to pass on what we have so far to Uncle Percy,' Jack replied, 'so could you and Teddy come to lunch in Watford tomorrow? Percy said he'd be awaiting confirmation of a meeting, and Polly has a leg of lamb that she's keen to convert into Sunday lunch.'

CHAPTER EIGHT

'Before or after dinner?' Jack asked of Percy as they sat with their drinks in the sitting room the following day, with the alluring aroma of roast lamb drifting through the slightly open door. The children had been banished to the garden, and Beattie was about to round them up and ensure that they scrubbed their hands before they were fed sausages in the kitchen.

'I'd regard it as a blessing if you'd leave all the cloak-and-dagger nonsense until *after* dinner,' she said sternly, 'since by then I'll be safely out of earshot in the park grounds with the children. And if you want Percy at his most underhanded, then he's best on a full stomach, I've noticed. At least I get to see the children more often these days, now that he seems to have dragged almost the entire family into another of his devious activities.'

After lunch, with two pots of tea on the low table between them, Percy, Jack, Esther and Lucy sat down to discuss their findings.

'Well, what have you got for me in connection with my latest "devious activity"?' Percy asked.

'I have to begin by saying what a wonderful actor Jack turned out to be,' Lucy enthused. 'I know he's my brother and all that, but I've seen a good number of superb actors in my time, and even if he hadn't slid into the auditions for a secret reason, he'd have got the part on sheer merit.'

'He had me reduced to tears,' Esther confessed, 'and the other actors seemed impressed, which is of course a good sign.'

'This is all very interesting, but let's not forget why you were there,' Percy cut in. 'What, if anything, did you learn that might shed light on how Valentine Primrose came to be murdered?'

'There was an extra knife,' Esther revealed.

It fell silent for a moment before Percy asked, 'When, and where?'

'On the table, following the entrance of the actors on stage for the assassination scene,' Esther replied. 'I got talking to a young woman called Alice Bennett, who like me is an assistant stage manager at the theatre. She was waiting in the kitchen for the props table to be emptied of knives when she heard an argument of sorts about who was to pick up which. So far as she could recall, that argument was between Ernest Graves and Simon Abelman, although it seems that Leopold Carter was there as well. Then when she went in there after the actors went on stage, she found a spare knife lying there. So there must have been six on the table when the five actors were picking up one each, and apparently arguing over who was to take which.'

'Did she report this to the police, and what did she do with the spare knife?' Percy demanded as his eyes widened with excitement.

'There was nothing in the police report, so far as I can recall,' said Jack.

'The knife must have gone back into the props cupboard, because when I went in there to get a spare with which to demonstrate to Inspector Buxton how the retraction mechanism worked, there were three to choose from,' said Lucy. 'There were eight originally, so if five went on stage, then the sixth one must have been put back in the cupboard. I'd be prepared to believe that Alice did that, because she wouldn't have wanted it to be left on the table while she laid out the refreshments, and it certainly wasn't there when I came back into the dressing room with the inspector.'

Percy thought for a moment, then asked, 'Is anyone else thinking what I'm thinking?'

'I gave it some thought when Esther told me about it on the way home,' Jack replied, 'and the presence of a sixth knife suggests to me that someone had acquired the additional one from the cupboard while no-one was looking, then put Lucy's hatpin into it ahead of the rest of the knives being put onto the table.'

'My thoughts exactly,' Percy confirmed with a smile, 'but that raises other important questions, does it not? Such as who put the remaining five knives onto the table, who had access to the props cupboard, who was able to acquire Lucy's hatpin and insert it into the sixth knife in advance, how did it get onto the table, and did anyone notice that there were six knives when there should have been only five?'

'I can answer some of those questions,' Lucy replied. 'The props cupboard is normally kept locked, and has only two keys. I have one, and at that time Alice Bennett would have had the other, since it was her job to put out the props for when they were needed. I found five knives lying on the props table in the middle of the dressing room just before the end of Act Two, as there should have been, and I checked each one for safety. If there was a sixth knife that had been sabotaged, then that explains how poor old Val came to be stabbed despite my efforts, and surely proves my innocence?'

'Once we prove the existence of the sixth knife, certainly,' Percy agreed, 'but what about your hatpin?'

Lucy frowned. 'That was probably my fault, although I hardly expected my hat to become a murder weapon. There's a coat stand in one corner of the dressing room, a large one to accommodate everyone's outer clothing when they come in from the street. I always hung my coat on it, and given the rather stuffy warmth of that changing room when we're all gathered in it, I would frequently pop my hat onto the brass knob at the top. My garden hat is particularly cumbersome once you're indoors, given the silk flowers all over it, so it was normal for it to be sitting there once I'd arrived for rehearsals. Then when we moved onto the stage for the rehearsal proper, anyone could have had access to it.'

'But surely you would have noticed if the pin had been removed when you came to put the hat back on?' Percy pressed.

Lucy shrugged. 'Not necessarily, even though it was one of my favourites that was stolen. I use more than one hatpin at a time, you see, and if rehearsals had run late I might have been in a hurry to get home. Teddy often let me use the coach for evening rehearsals, rather than letting me walk the streets in the dark, and I hated to keep Thomas waiting. Sometimes I didn't even bother putting my hat back on, since I'd be jumping straight into the waiting coach, and then into the house a few minutes later.'

'But there was never a time when you noticed that the hatpin was missing?' Percy asked.

She shook her head. 'When Buxton showed it to me and asked me to identify it, I must have assumed that it had fallen off onto the dressing room floor. Had I known that it had been used in the murder, I might have thought twice about owning up to it being mine.'

'It speaks volumes for your innocence that you didn't even attempt to deny it,' Percy replied consolingly. 'But what can anyone else tell me about the rehearsal yesterday, if anything?'

'Simon Abelman easily accepted that I'd got the part of Laertes,' Jack reported.

'That's because he landed the plum lead role of Hamlet,' Lucy reminded him. 'Every actor's fondest ambition is to play Hamlet. And all the actors seem to accept you as one of their number, not just Simon.'

'Particularly that unpleasant Graves chap.' Jack shuddered. 'I think he may prefer the company of men, as Percy hinted, given the number of times he found an excuse to put his sweaty hand on my arm.'

'But he was fulsome in his praise of your acting ability,' Esther put in. 'Even that rather dowdy Alice Bennett seemed anxious to make your further acquaintance.'

'Which is all to the good,' said Percy, 'since she may be the key to us discovering, step by step, what really happened that night.'

'Well, if she makes any more obvious ploys to get Jack's attention, I can't guarantee that I won't scupper all our plans by smacking her across the mouth,' Esther said with a pout.

Jack laughed. 'You're clearly expecting me to be patient while you work your charm on Simon Abelman,' he said, 'so you'll just have to grit your teeth while I see what Alice can tell me.'

'Have you made any progress with Simon, Esther?' Percy asked.

Esther nodded. 'He seems to have bought the idea that I'm one of those women who're determined to get more power and prestige in society. He thinks it might be a good idea for me to meet his lady friend Florence, or "Flo", as he calls her.'

'Excellent!' Percy said with satisfaction. 'Keep that up, and try to drag Lucy in with you. We don't want you going into WSPU territory on your own.'

'What else do you want me to do?' Lucy asked.

'Tell me more about anyone who might have gained access to the key to the props cupboard.'

'Well, mine was always kept in my costume jacket pocket,' Lucy insisted, 'but I can't be absolutely certain that Alice didn't loan hers to anyone, if they gave her a reasonable excuse for needing it.'

'Or if they had some other means of persuading her to hand it over,' Percy mused. 'Bribery, threats, blackmail — something along those lines.'

'Alice Bennett?' Lucy replied sceptically. 'I can't imagine for one moment that she was ever guilty of behaviour that could lead to that. Mind you, she does on occasion give me the impression that she has an eye for our leading stagehand — to be honest, our *only* stagehand — a young man called Joseph Banks, who doesn't have any theatrical ambitions, but just works for a pound a day whenever we need him. I think he's in need of the money, with a sick mother living somewhere down in Shoreditch or somewhere like that. And he might have a legitimate reason to require the key anyway, since he's the one who has to do the placing of props onstage, under Alice's immediate supervision. I have the ultimate responsibility for stage management, obviously, but I have to delegate some of it while I'm also producing and directing.'

'We might need to take a closer look at him,' Percy told Jack, 'since a person in need of immediate cash might be susceptible to a bribe. Our quarry may have prevailed upon him to request the props cupboard key from Alice, then hand it over briefly.'

'I'll do what I can,' Jack promised, 'but bear in mind that I have to keep up the pretence of being an ambitious actor. And even though my part is a relatively short one, with my appearances on stage coming in bursts, I still need to concentrate on learning my lines.'

*

The first rehearsal was scheduled for the following tuesday. Given Esther's need to hold together the teaching programme at Cassiobury House School during the continued illness of its headmistress and proprietor, Emily Allsop, it was agreed that Esther would not attend the midweek evening rehearsals, putting in an appearance only at the Saturday one. Jack, on the other hand, would continue in his assumed role of an enthusiastic and gifted actor, attending both evening rehearsals and staying overnight with Percy and Beattie in Hackney.

The first Tuesday rehearsal was a line reading of Act One, with the relevant actors seated in a circle in the dressing room as they read through their lines, each of them armed with a copy of the script. The arrangement, as ever, was that the weekday evenings would be dedicated to line rehearsals, with Lucy offering the occasional direction regarding how the lines should be delivered and reading the minor parts for which there was as yet no actor. Saturday would be dedicated to stage direction, or "blocking", as Lucy called it, much to Jack's confusion.

Jack was therefore puzzled as to why both Alice Bennett and Joe Banks were present at the Tuesday evening rehearsal, since they had no more need to be there than Esther. He could only assume that they had nothing better to do, and that Joe at least was keen to attend in order to earn his pound a day.

But another reason suggested itself when they wound up their first read-through at around nine o'clock, and Alice sidled up to Jack as they were donning their coats.

'A few of us normally nip down to the Lamb and Flag in Covent Garden after rehearsals,' she said quietly. 'It's only a few streets away, in Rose Street. Would you care to join us?'

When he appeared hesitant, she lowered her voice even more and added, 'You'd be doing me a great favour if you'd agree.'

Jack was in two minds. On the one hand he was reluctant to do anything that might be misconstrued by Esther, and was anxious not to give Alice the idea that he might be interested in a relationship with her. But he'd taken on this acting role in the hope of learning more about the circumstances of Valentine Primrose's murder, and given that there would be a group of them walking a few streets away for a more relaxed, and perhaps unguarded, social gathering, it might be a good opportunity to acquire some information. With some lingering reservations, he agreed.

'This is awfully good of you,' Alice enthused as she took his arm and led the way, several of the actors both ahead of and behind them. 'I have an ulterior motive,' she admitted as she edged closer. 'I'm trying to make Joe jealous, in the hope that he pays me a little more attention.'

Now it began to make sense. Joe Banks needed the money, and Alice was anxious to attract Joe's attention. There was no harm in going along with this temporary ruse, and earning Alice's gratitude in the hope that she'd be more forthcoming with information about the fatal night. A few drinks might loosen a tongue or two.

When they reached the Lamb and Flag, they took their places in what Alice told Jack was their usual corner. Jack found himself seated next to Leopold Carter, a rather nervous little man who seemed to shun the company of the louder actors, led by a somewhat flamboyant Simon Abelman. Simon insisted on buying drinks for himself, Henry Gloucester and Arthur Dennistoun, thus implicitly snubbing Jack, Alice, Joe and Leopold. Jack was about to offer to buy a drink for those who had been left out when to his amazement Joe Banks got in ahead of him. Was this the same man who Lucy believed only came to theatre rehearsals because he was desperate to earn a pound for every attendance? Percy would obviously need to be told of this, because something clearly wasn't quite right.

No sooner were the drinks on the table than Alice turned to Joe and engaged him in a conversation that sounded to Jack's untutored ears as if it related to stage management. Joe paid attention but there was no warmth in his look, and Jack could tell that he was bored. His eyes occasionally flickered across to Jack and Leopold, as if silently seeking rescue. In order to divert both of them from the slight embarrassment of watching Alice showing a little too much enthusiasm, Jack turned to Leopold and said the first thing that came into his head.

'I must say that I think you're very brave, going back on stage again after what must have been a terrible trauma for you.'

'The part of Horatio's a fairly minor one, of course,' Leopold reminded him, 'and Lucy was very good in giving me a part that's not too taxing, and doesn't involve knives, thank God.'

'I can well imagine how holding a knife on stage would bring back awful memories,' Jack prompted.

Leopold's eyes began to water as he nodded. 'Val was such a good friend too, so it was doubly traumatic for me. One of those horrible curses of Fate, I suppose, since I took the only knife that was left. Serves me right for giving in to my weak stomach.'

'I'm sorry?' Jack replied, unsure what the connection might be.

Leopold lowered his voice. 'I've always been a nervous type,' he admitted, 'which is why I took up acting, really. A doctor friend of mine recommended it in order to build up my self-confidence. But just before I go on stage, I always need to visit the lavatory, and that night was no different. When I got back to the dressing room, Simon was waiting for me, and yelling that I was keeping them all from going onstage after the interval. There was one knife left on the table, and he urged me to grab it and get onstage without any further delay. So I did, and as luck would have it, that was the knife whose blade stuck.'

'So you got the last knife?' Jack asked in case he'd misheard.

Leopold nodded. 'I was the last one to go onstage, and there were five knives for five actors, so *obviously* it was the last one. Simon must have taken the one before that. If I hadn't had to make that final trip to the lavatory, he might have got the one that killed poor old Val.'

There were now tears rolling down his cheeks, and Joe was looking at him with curiosity. 'What's up, Leo?' he asked, no doubt trying to escape Alice's undivided attention.

'Nothing,' Leopold replied as he took a deep breath and brushed his hand across his cheeks. 'I was just telling young Jack here about how Fate dealt me the knife that killed Val. It was the only one left, and it serves me right that I was the one doomed to wield it.'

Jack looked hastily at Alice's face and saw the confusion in her eyes. He took a great risk as he said, 'You obviously sympathise with Leo, as I'm sure we all can.'

'It's not that,' she murmured. 'It's just that — well, perhaps I was mistaken, but I thought there was a knife left behind when they all went onstage.'

'How could that be?' Jack asked as innocently as he could. 'Five actors, and five knives, surely? Are you saying that there was a sixth one? It wouldn't have affected the outcome, since obviously the one that Leo picked up was the defective one.'

'Yes,' said Alice, 'I must have got it wrong, I suppose. Just goes to show that your memory can sometimes play you false.'

After an hour or so the small party began to break up, Leopold making his excuses and leaving when he saw Simon and Arthur doing the same. This left Henry Gloucester, who offered to escort Alice to her bus stop. When she looked enquiringly at Joe, he hastily told her that he had to get home to Shoreditch to make sure his mother didn't need anything before her bedtime. Jack left a few paces behind Joe and was surprised to note that, far from heading for a bus that would take him into the East End, he walked in the opposite direction, clearly intent on making his way further into Covent Garden, or even Soho. Jack slid from doorway to doorway, so that when Joe looked round nervously from time to time, he was unaware that his furtive actions had been noted.

Back in Hackney, Percy was waiting up for Jack with a welcoming whisky. 'Anything of interest to me?' he asked.

'Most definitely,' said Jack. 'That Joe Banks isn't what he pretends to be. He's not poor, and I doubt very much whether he has a sick mother in Shoreditch. The actors and stage people go for a drink after the evening rehearsals, and I've just come from the Lamb and Flag, in Covent Garden, where Joe spent more on drinks than he'd earned all evening.'

'I'll need to look more carefully at him, as I already predicted,' Percy said with a smile. 'When you go for drinks on Thursday evening I'll follow you all, and if you can find some way of identifying Joe, I'll follow him to where he goes afterwards. Anything else?'

'Yes. According to Leo Carter, the fatal knife was the last one left on the table — the last of five, he recalls. He was sort of hurried into taking it by Simon Abelman, and that raises the interesting question of why Alice Bennett recalled a spare knife when she went to lay out the refreshments.'

'Interesting,' Percy muttered thoughtfully. 'When you go home to Esther tomorrow evening, tell her what you just told me and ask her to prompt Alice's memory again.'

'Won't we be at risk of making ourselves too obvious?'

'Yes, but it'll be a risk worth taking, if, as I suspect, Abelman had two knives in his possession when Carter took the fifth, and fatal one, and Abelman needed to discard one of them. Well done, Jack. I sense that the net's beginning to tighten.'

CHAPTER NINE

Esther sensed immediately that something was wrong as she looked up from the entrance gates to Cassiobury House School and saw a serious-faced middle-aged man waiting for her in its doorway. Urging Lily and Annabelle to run ahead of her and join their playmates in the schoolyard, she walked up to the man with a sinking feeling.

'Mrs Enright?' the man asked.

Esther nodded, somehow unable to force a word from her tightening throat.

'I'm Dr Bainbridge, and I've just come down from visiting Miss Allsop. It's bad news, I'm afraid.'

'Is she — has she…? I mean…'

'No, she's still alive, but very ill. I'm afraid it's tuberculosis.'

'Dear God,' Esther gasped as tears welled in her eyes. 'How long…? I mean — well, you know…'

'There can be no way of telling,' the doctor replied. 'If she were able to enter a sanatorium in Switzerland or somewhere, perhaps indefinitely, although that would not be an existence that anyone would welcome. But she insists that she must remain here and see to the welfare of her pupils, and the future of the school that she's dedicated her life to. And she's a very determined lady, as you probably know.'

'Indeed,' Esther confirmed. 'Is she up to receiving visitors?'

'You, anyway,' he replied. 'She asked that I wait here for you and explain the situation. Then she wishes you to go up and speak with her.'

'Yes, of course,' Esther choked out through her tears. 'Just as soon as I've got classes underway.'

Forty minutes later, having set both classes some exercises to complete in her absence, she went up the stairs to Emily's private quarters, and called out cheerily as she made her way down the short hallway and entered Emily's bedroom. 'Only me, as instructed. The children have been left with enough to keep them busy until the mid-morning break, so I thought I'd come up and bother you.'

'No bother, dear Esther, and let's not pretend with each other,' Emily croaked, then gave way to a fit of coughing. Esther hurried to the side of the bed, and tried not to show her shock as she looked down at a face as white as chalk. Emily's still piercing blue eyes stood out like icicles.

'Sit beside me and listen carefully, while I still have breath,' Emily instructed her hoarsely as she dabbed her lips with a kerchief already soiled with blood. 'First and foremost, I've arranged for a relief teacher to be sent from the East Ham Training College where you gained your accreditation. Miss Doris Walker will be arriving by the end of the week to take over the combined junior class while you continue with the seniors. Then I'd like you to take over my responsibilities for recruitment, parental inspections and so on. The school must go on, and there's no-one else I trust more than you to maintain the programme I've established here. It will be my legacy, no doubt before many more months have passed.'

'Please, Emily, don't talk like that!' Esher pleaded as she began to sob, and laid her head on Emily's cold hand where it lay exposed on the bedcover.

'I'm being practical, as usual,' Emily insisted. 'The school must go on, regardless of the health of its headmistress, and the important thing is the ongoing tuition of the pupils downstairs. I'll be relying on you, so don't let me down, please.'

'Of *course* I won't let you down, dear, *dear* Emily!' Esther sobbed. 'I owe you *so* much!'

'So go back down there and show me *how* much,' Emily insisted as she attempted a smile, then continued coughing helplessly.

'Can I get you something — tea, your medicine, brandy?' Esther pleaded.

Emily shook her head and waved her away, managing one word between coughs: 'Downstairs!'

Somehow Esther survived that day, followed by the next, and on Wednesday morning the caretaker, Bentinck, was waiting for her in the hallway as the pupils scampered out for their mid-morning break.

'There's a lady outside who says she's expected,' he told her in his somewhat deferential manner. 'Name of Walker.'

'Ah yes, Doris Walker,' Esther replied as she looked down the hall towards the front door. Waiting for her was a stout woman in her mid-thirties with a heavy travelling bag, watching the children as they rushed past, shouting and laughing.

'You must be Mrs Enright,' the woman said with a smile as she turned towards Esther. 'I was told to ask for you, and here I am.'

'Do you know why you've been asked to assist here?' Esther asked.

'Only that the headmistress is unwell and temporarily unable to assume her teaching duties.'

'She's unlikely to be able to do so for a long time,' Esther replied sadly, 'so when can you commence duties, and do you have somewhere to stay?'

'I've taken a room in a boarding house down the road that was recommended by the college,' Doris replied, 'but I also have a cousin who lives in Bushey, so if there's an omnibus service to and from there to here, that won't be a problem. And I can start today, if that's convenient for you.'

'Definitely,' Esther replied. 'I'd like you to assume responsibility for Primaries One and Two, which are combined, with a total of seventeen pupils. I'll then be able to resume fulltime duties with the combined senior class, which has been sadly neglected in recent weeks. Miss Allsop has also asked me to accept temporary responsibilities as Headmistress, so you'll be reporting to me. Once Bentinck — he's the caretaker — rings the bell, and the pupils line up to return to class, I'll introduce you to them all, and you can accompany them back into class. We can meet up again during the lunch break.'

Jack was reluctant to leave Esther on the Thursday morning, given her ongoing grief regarding Emily's declining health, but he had his duties to attend to at the Yard, and in the evening Percy was expecting him to identify Joe Banks as they left rehearsals. Jack didn't really need to be at this rehearsal, given that his character didn't appear in the portion of Act One that they were reading through, but it gave him more time to study Joe and Alice from under lowered eyelids, wondering how much, if anything, Alice really knew about the young man whose eye she was so anxious to catch.

Shortly after nine that evening, as the small group made their way to the Lamb and Flag, Jack held back slightly, looking anxiously about. To his left was what appeared to be an elderly newspaper seller huddling in a doorway, and in the belief that this was another of Uncle Percy's disguises, he called out loudly, 'Joe — slow down a bit, so that I can catch up!'

Joe obligingly looked back towards Jack, and without slackening his pace called back in reply, 'Last one there buys the drinks!' He then turned to continue his furtive conversation with Ernest Graves. Jack looked enquiringly at the shabby old man in the doorway, who gave a sharp nod to confirm that he now knew who Joe Banks was, and Jack scuttled across the street to rejoin the group.

An hour later Joe was the first to leave the pub, and Percy emerged from the alleyway across the road in order to follow him, discarding his disguise as a newspaper seller and instead pretending to be a working man on his way to or from his job as he dogged along fifty yards behind the man he was tailing.

He was beginning to doubt the wisdom of trying to follow a young man in an obvious hurry as they passed quickly down narrow lanes that crossed first Garrick Street, then St Martin's Lane, to emerge finally in Charing Cross Road. Joe turned sharply north for several hundred yards, then led Percy through another set of increasingly sordid alleys in Soho until they came to Old Compton Street. Percy was obliged to duck hastily into a darkened bookseller's doorway when Joe stopped and looked both ways before crossing the street and knocking four times on an innocuous-looking door. A hatch opened in the top of the door, and Joe appeared to converse briefly with the man whose face appeared in the frame. The door was opened for long enough for Joe to slip inside, then hastily closed again.

Percy's best guess at this stage was that the premises that Joe had entered was some sort of private club. Given the reputation of Soho in general, and Old Compton Street in particular, he could well imagine what sort of facilities the club offered. Whatever they were, they'd be well beyond the resources of the working-class man with a sick mother that Joe was pretending to be.

Percy crossed the road and surveyed the rather weatherworn blue door with its peeling paint and the slightly fresher black lettering above the hatch that identified the establishment as "Poppy's". Imitating the actions that he'd observed while watching Joe, he rapped on the door four times, and in due course the hatch at the top of it opened to reveal a metal grille with a man's face behind it. Not the friendliest face Percy had ever encountered, nor the most closely shaven, but then doorkeepers employed at Soho clubs were not hired for the quality of their personal grooming.

'Whaddya want?' the man asked gruffly.

Percy extracted a five pound note from his wallet, waved it in front of the man's face, then folded it in such a way that it could be passed through the grille.

'I wish to purchase five pounds worth of information regarding how one becomes a member of "Poppy's",' he said with a smile.

'Yer comes back 'ere wiv fifty quid, an' yer asks nicely,' the man replied gruffly. 'Mind, yer'd prob'ly need ter be a lot younger ter be allowed in 'ere. An' a lot prettier.'

'Thank you kindly,' Percy replied as he released the money into the man's eager grip, turned, and walked back across Old Compton Street with a broad smile.

It wouldn't be the first time he and Jack had investigated a molly house.

'Absolutely and definitely not!' Jack insisted when Percy revealed his findings and suggested their next possible move. He'd waited up for Percy's return, and the two of them were now consuming whisky in the sitting room of the Hackney house. It was approaching midnight, and Jack had been dozing in front of the dying fire when Percy returned with his news.

'Do you have any better ideas?' Percy demanded.

Jack shook his head. 'No. I'm just saying that there's no way I'm going to set foot in that club.'

'And I don't suppose you'd be prepared to call for all the files on raided molly houses in London in the faint hope that the name "Joe Banks" turns up, either?'

'Again, definitely not.'

'Not even under the pretence that you have your suspicions regarding an applicant for recruitment into the Met?'

'Not even for that.'

'Then what bloody use are you to me in the task that we've set ourselves to prove Lucy's innocence?'

'Haven't I already gone through the trauma of trying to be an actor, learning lines, insinuating myself into a theatre group full of poseurs, dragging Esther in along with me, and identifying Joe Banks? Incidentally, you may find that Esther isn't quite up to playing her role either, given the extra burden she's been obliged to take on because Emily Allsop's gone down with TB. So don't push your luck.'

'If I were to acquire a photograph of Banks, would you at least be prepared to circulate it around the Met, in case anyone can shed light on his true identity?'

'I suppose I could manage that,' Jack agreed grudgingly, 'but I don't know how to handle one of those camera things.'

'You won't have to,' Percy told him, 'since I can find someone else to do that. What I'll need is a decent excuse, and I hope that your sister will prove to be more obliging than you've been. Might I suggest another Sunday lunch in Watford this coming weekend? Hopefully Esther will be able to report progress in the matter of cosying up to Simon Abelman. Now, it's time for bed, before you get even grumpier.'

*

When the theatre group members began arriving for their first Saturday rehearsal, they found Esther seated at the props table, a collection of assorted Tudor costumes in a pile to one side, and a heavily brocaded royal gown in her busy hands as she worked on fixing a seam that had come undone. Lucy was seated at her side, chatting away happily, while Jack was pacing up and down, murmuring his Act One lines under his breath.

Once everyone had assembled, Lucy called them to order and announced, 'We'll be keeping it as simple as possible for this next production, and we would seem to have enough basic doublet and hose for the main characters. As you can see, Esther is putting her excellent needlework skills to good use as she repairs the gown that I'll be wearing as Queen Gertrude. Over the coming weeks she'll make her way through our somewhat frayed collection, and that will be her main function, while Alice and Joe will join me in stage direction. So let's go next door onto the stage, and work on the blocking for the opening scene, shall we?'

Once the relevant characters had assembled on the stage, with Lucy standing slightly below them in front of the first row of audience seats with Alice, Lucy went on, 'I've taken the liberty of cutting Scene One, so we open with the court scene. Claudius, grab a chair and sit upstage at the centre, where I'll be joining you in due course. The rest of you line up stage right — Laertes to the front — as if queuing for service at your local baker's shop. Hamlet, stand on the other side, looking disapprovingly at your stepfather's usurpation of your dead father's throne, and his marriage to your mother. And — go!'

For two hours they repeated the same short scene, in which Jack delivered his only speech from memory, kneeling in front of Henry Gloucester, while the remainder of the main characters read from their heavily edited scripts. Lucy and

Alice called out the lines for the missing characters who would be acquired from local theatre companies in due course. When they adjourned for the lunch break, Alice scuttled into the kitchen and brought out the tray of sandwiches that she'd made in advance, while Esther put the pot on to boil and laid out the teacups, having cleared the props tables of the costumes that she'd been working on.

As they munched happily on cheese and tomato sandwiches, Lucy gave her opinion that the scene had gone well. 'I was particularly impressed that Jack had committed his lines to memory,' she said, 'but the rest of you will need to leave your scripts aside the next time we run through that scene.'

'All very well, unless you have as much to remember as I do,' Simon grumbled.

Lucy smiled encouragingly. 'It's the burden of taking the lead role, Simon. There's more to *Hamlet* than "To be or not to be", remember.'

'It felt awkward with so many of the minor characters missing,' Henry complained. 'Can we not at least get our borrowed Rosencrantz and Guildenstern over here for rehearsals?'

'Not yet,' Lucy replied. 'I don't want to stretch their generosity to the point at which they withdraw their generous offers to assist.'

'How about at least getting Alice, Esther and Joe to stand in for them during rehearsals?' Simon suggested.

Alice nodded eagerly. 'I'd *love* that!' she enthused.

'How would you two feel about that?' Lucy asked Esther and Joe.

'Count me in,' Joe replied.

Esther shrugged. 'I have enough to do sewing all these costumes, some of which are hanging by a mere thread. And as much as I'd like to progress with my career in the theatre, I don't think I could do two jobs at once.'

'That's precisely the lack of ambition that keeps women held down in modern society!' Simon objected. 'This is your first opportunity to stand up for yourself and realise your aspirations, and you're responding like a scared little mouse who just saw a big cat approaching. Next Saturday I'll bring my lady friend Flo along, and she'll give you lessons in how to stand up for yourself in this man's world.'

'I don't need lessons from *anyone*, thank you!' Esther protested loudly. 'And keep your condescending advice to yourself!'

Simon grinned. 'You *definitely* need to meet Flo. You've got her spirit already; all you need is a little encouragement to take your chances when they arise. Lucy, I take it that Flo would be allowed to attend next Saturday's rehearsals?'

'Of course,' Lucy agreed. 'While she's at it, she can read some of the parts that Henry was complaining about. But next Tuesday we start on Act One, Scene Three, so Jack, start learning your lines for the farewell scene with Ophelia and Polonius. Perhaps we'll get Alice to read Ophelia's lines. Or perhaps Esther, since Hamlet seems to have appointed himself as her patron.'

CHAPTER TEN

'It's been an interesting week for me,' Percy observed, once Beattie had left the room in order to supervise the children washing their hands ahead of Sunday lunch in the Watford house. 'But before I go into that, what can the rest of you tell me?'

'Well,' Esther began, 'I think I'm about to be introduced to Florence Bannister, thanks to Simon Abelman swallowing my bait.'

Jack gave a low growl. 'Patronising bastard that he is! He seems to think that he knows all there is to know about women's rights as *well* as acting. And from what I could tell, his acting's not of the finest either.'

'Unless you want to play Hamlet yourself,' Lucy replied firmly, 'I strongly advise against antagonising him to the point at which he walks out on us. You're constantly complaining about having to learn your lines — which, incidentally, you seem to have mastered very well — but the part of Hamlet would test anyone's memory, so give him some sympathy and play to his ego.'

'Anyone else?' Percy asked. The others shook their heads, so he puffed out his cheeks in self-congratulation as he announced, 'Well, I can add something to our general knowledge. Something that only Jack knows at present.'

'Joe Banks prefers the company of men,' said Jack, 'and after our Thursday evening meeting, Percy followed him to a molly house.'

'Translation, please,' Lucy requested, 'for the benefit of those of us not familiar with the more mysterious side of London life.'

'A molly house is where homosexual men meet,' said Percy. 'Jack in particular became very familiar with at least one of those some years ago, when we were tasked with enquiring into the private life of a man who was one of England's most admired playwrights at that time. Lucy at least will have heard of Oscar Wilde.'

'Indeed I have,' said Lucy. 'We successfully staged his *Lady Windermere's Fan* a few years ago. But didn't he go to prison for something or other?'

'The "something or other" was his sexual orientation,' Percy told her.

'Are you telling us that Joe Banks is similarly inclined?' Lucy asked.

'Why else would he be visiting a molly house?' Percy replied.

'It would, of course, partly explain why he hasn't fallen for the blandishments of Miss Bennett,' Jack added.

'You mean because he's otherwise inclined?' Teddy asked.

Jack nodded, adding, 'That, plus the fact that she's a bit lumpy and drab.'

Esther hissed quietly. 'Is that how women are destined to be judged, solely by their looks?' she demanded. 'How about their personalities and their abilities? Alice strikes me as the perfect life companion for the right man, given her warmth, her sincerity, and her willingness to undertake mundane tasks while others enjoy the spotlight.'

'Save your sermon for Simon Abelman's soapbox,' Jack replied hotly.

Percy raised a hand in order to regain everyone's attention. 'I'd like to make a suggestion or two about how we proceed with what we have so far. I think that my sensitive nose just detected an increased aroma of roast beef, which suggests that Polly has just extracted our dinner from the oven, and will shortly be dispatching it to the dining room. When that happens, we'll need to talk about mundane things for Beattie's benefit, so hear me out.'

It fell respectfully silent as Percy explained, 'There's clearly more to Joe Banks than meets the eye. Apart from anything else, he shares the same sexual preferences as not only Leopold Carter, who resided with the deceased Valentine Primrose, but also Primrose himself. Jack and I need a photograph of him, so that Jack can ask around the Met if anyone knows him by sight. If someone can come up with his real name, we might be able to get somewhere. So I've devised a strategy for obtaining that photograph.' He smiled. 'Meet Francis Pierrepoint, writer and journalist.'

'You, presumably?' Jack asked.

'My good self indeed,' Percy confirmed. 'Next Saturday I propose that I arrive at your rehearsal, posing as a journalist and writer specialising in the theatre who's keen to sell a feature to the London newspapers about a dedicated amateur theatre group that has soldiered on despite a lack of patronage, and in the face of falling volunteer numbers.'

'That certainly sounds like us,' Lucy conceded, 'but where does photography come into it?'

'Don't you ever read the daily papers? All the leading stories are supported — "enhanced", if you prefer — by photographs,' said Percy. 'The most popular are the ones with photographs all over them, because they appeal to people who can't read. There's also that new one — the *Illustrated London News* — that specialises in them, in order to attract a healthy readership. You *must* remember how even the highbrow newspapers couldn't resist printing a picture of Victoria when she died a few years ago. Only a few weeks ago we were treated to images of Russian soldiers firing at protestors.'

'Point taken, Percy,' Teddy interrupted him. 'So you intend on taking a photograph of the entire theatre, along with its leading cast members, in order to get a clear image of this "Joe Banks" fellow?'

'Precisely. I'll even push my luck and ask each individual member to pose for a head and shoulders image, so that I end up with a good one of Banks.'

'But from what I remember from our wedding day,' Lucy objected, 'each photograph takes minutes to produce, with someone standing under a black cover and exhorting everyone not to move. You'll use up our entire rehearsal time, surely?'

Percy chuckled and tapped his nose. 'It may have been like that in those days, but the science has moved on. I've tentatively acquired the services of an old colleague of mine who, instead of retiring into a private enquiry agency such as mine, developed his former hobby interest in photography, and he showed me this little box on which you just press a button. The film inside can be "developed", as they call it, inside his workshop, and within several days I'll have the image I need to establish Banks's real identity. All I need is your co-operation next Saturday.'

'If you say so,' Lucy agreed with obvious reservations, 'but could we arrange to do it during our normal lunchtime break? I want to attempt to stage three scenes from Act One for the rest of the day.'

'Bertie tells me that he's going to watch some real soldiers in action next week,' Beattie observed as she helped herself to Brussels sprouts from the dish in the centre of the lunch table.

Jack frowned deeply. 'Against my better judgment, I'm afraid. That jingoistic windbag Essex is training up young boys as the next generation of cannon fodder, and he regards Bertie as a prize catch, taking advantage of his lifelong interest in anything military, and boosting his enthusiasm by giving him corporal's stripes. I'm fearful that if another war breaks out, and the Reserve regiments are mobilised, boys like Bertie will be encouraged to sign up for the Volunteers as the next wave to be sent to wherever it's happening.'

'But surely the exercise is good for a boy of his age and restless temperament?' Beattie argued.

Jack snorted. 'They're already being issued with broom handles in order to practise drilling and marching up and down. The visit that Bertie was telling you about is to the Drill Hall here in Watford, where the Reserve Battalion of the Hertfordshire Regiment will be doing it with real rifles, no doubt with bayonets stuck on the end. Just the sort of thing likely to encourage an impressionable lad like Bertie.'

'Annabelle's doing really well in class, now that I've been able to leave the primary classes under the management of the new teacher,' Esther butted in before Jack got into his stride. 'And whatever Annabelle does, Lily copies, and vice versa, so it's been a double benefit having Doris Walker joining us.' Esther sighed. 'Emily's doctor doesn't hold out much hope if she's not able to enter some sort of sanatorium. Even then her prospects aren't good. I'm now effectively the headmistress, as well as acting as proprietor, showing prospective parents around the school, meeting with Government inspectors and suchlike.'

'Well, if there's anything I can do to lighten your load, just let me know,' Beattie offered. 'I'm more than happy to take on Miriam and Thomas as a sort of project of my own.'

'That's very good of you, Aunt Beattie,' Esther replied, 'and I won't hesitate to call on you if needs be.'

'Just don't let her give Miriam cookery lessons,' Percy muttered, and everyone fought to suppress their laughter.

'Allow me to introduce Francis Pierrepoint,' Lucy announced the following Saturday, as everyone began eagerly consuming the sandwiches brought into the theatre by Alice, and drinking the tea made by Esther. The blocking rehearsal of the whole of Act One had gone relatively smoothly, although Lucy was still not happy with the extent to which everyone had learned their lines, and it was now time to relax for an hour and take the weight off their weary feet.

'Mr Pierrepoint will hopefully bring us some much-needed publicity,' Lucy added, 'when he gets a story published in a leading London newspaper about the way we've kept the flag of amateur theatre flying despite the odds being against us. Perhaps it'll gain us more volunteers, and — dare we hope? — more financial support from eager patrons. So over to you, Francis.'

'I want to concentrate on the personal, human angle,' Percy explained as he feigned a somewhat effeminate voice and tried his best to look artistic. 'You know what I mean — "When did you first realise that you wanted to act? Why did you settle for an amateur career? What's the part you'd most like to play?" and so on. I can then match up each little biography with a photograph to be taken by my associate William Penny here, using the latest scientific miracle, the box camera. So let's start with the leading actor, shall we? The one playing Hamlet?'

Simon Abelman stood up with a self-conscious grin and announced, 'That will be me. I'm a barrister at law by profession, and obviously I earn much more in that capacity than I would as a professional actor. But there's a little bit of actor in every barrister, so it comes naturally to me.'

'Excellent!' Percy enthused. 'A perfect little vignette to start us off with. If you could just move in front of that white screen that Mr Penny's constructed, he can take a suitable photograph of you to appear above your little piece. Now, who's next?'

One by one the actors lined up to tell their brief life stories, and explain their interest in amateur theatricals. Jack listened intently while Ernest Graves explained, 'I work in a somewhat boring and repetitive Government post that, although classified as "confidential" and of "primary importance to the nation's security", is frightfully dull. Without being able to let myself unfold like a chrysalis in order to reveal my inner butterfly, I'd probably go quietly mad. So here I am, playing Polonius, an elderly man whose murder provokes a duel between the two main characters.'

'Again, a wonderful "catch" for my intended readers,' Percy murmured. 'A real-life spy playing a tragic undercover role.'

'I wouldn't exactly call myself a "spy",' Ernest objected. 'My work assists that of undercover operatives, certainly, but in reality the job is very humdrum and desk-bound.'

'I'll make it sound a good deal more romantic than that,' Percy promised him. 'Let Mr Penny take your photograph.'

It was early afternoon before they'd worked their way through the main cast members. The only ones remaining to be interviewed, if at all, were Joe, Alice and Esther. Lucy was impatient to continue with stage rehearsals, but Percy was insistent and pointed to Joe. 'What about you, young man? What part do you have in this upcoming play?'

'I don't,' Joe said with a pout, 'although one day I'd like to. I'm just part of the backstage team, fixing up scenery, ensuring that the right props are on stage, and sometimes helping with the lighting.'

'That's just as important as acting,' Percy insisted, 'so before Mr Penny records your face for posterity, tell me a little about yourself.'

'Nothing interesting to tell, really,' Joe insisted modestly. 'I take clerical work when I can get it, because I was fortunate enough to get a modest education, before my father died of a fever. Now I just bumble along working in insurance offices and the like, and I look after my old mother, who's not too good on her feet these days. She lives on an upper floor in a residential block in Bethnal Green.'

'A story to touch the heart,' Percy murmured appreciatively. 'My readers will love it. Mr Penny, please give this noble young man the benefit of your best attention.'

When it came to Jack, he gave the pre-prepared story about his blossoming professional practice in insurance broking, and his introduction to the exciting new world of theatre through a professional association with Lucy's husband, Edward Masefield. He smiled for the box camera, and while he was doing that it was Alice's turn to tell her story, while Lucy made a pretence of being irritated by how long it was all taking.

Alice's story was even more depressing than Joe's. She'd been orphaned at the age of nine, then brought up in the Holborn Union Workhouse until she'd been discharged at the age of fourteen to work in a local laundry, before moving on to her current position in the kitchens of a bakery in Farringdon. She was now twenty-four years old, and hopeful of becoming an actress of sorts and finding a young man.

The last in line was Esther. In accordance with the pre-agreed script that had been carefully worked out the previous Sunday, Percy opened with, 'Finally, the lady whose physical beauty would light up any theatre, regardless of whatever mundane tasks she conducts in order to keep the main actors in the spotlight.'

'Don't patronise me, you slimy bastard!' Esther spat back. 'And tell your performing monkey Penny where he can shove his camera!'

'I beg your pardon?' Percy replied with feigned shock and outrage.

'Just because I'm a woman, and I held back to let the others make their bid for fame ahead of me, you assumed that I'm one of those timid little mice who's content to sit in the background in return for the occasional pat on the head. Well, let me tell you something, you snivelling little poseur — women make the world go round so that men can take the credit. Without women to massage men's egos, give them children, cook their meals, and sew their clothes, the world would quickly grind to a halt. Don't bother asking what I do around here, because it probably isn't as interesting to your readers — assuming that you ever get any! I'm off back to my kitchen, so go back to your playpen!'

Percy pretended to look stunned, then turned to Penny. 'Come on, Bill, it's clearly time we left. This young lady apparently doesn't need any assistance from us to decide how to conduct her life.'

'But she'd benefit from some guidance from me,' remarked the young woman who'd arrived in time to be introduced to the lunchtime gathering as Simon Abelman's "young lady", Florence Bannister. She'd been a silent observer of all that had so far transpired, but now she leapt into life like a horse released from a stable without a halter. 'That's *precisely* how to deal with the condescension and arrogant assumptions of men — politicians in particular! If we all reacted to being held down the way you just did — even though you were perhaps missing an opportunity for advancement on a man's terms — then society would be much healthier, and the nation better governed. Would you be interested in meeting with a group of women who think exactly as you do?'

'How many?' Esther asked in what she hoped was a convincingly naive tone of voice.

'Dozens, possibly hundreds. And *thousands* once we get our message out there! *Do* please join us tomorrow afternoon in Caxton Hall — that's in Westminster, and we hire it for our larger meetings. There are some ladies there who you should meet without delay. You'll find that they think just as you do, and are committed to ending male dominance over our way of life. We're well on the way to seeing women playing an equal role in society to that of men. *Do* please promise to come — Simon can collect you from wherever you live, and walk you down there.'

'I know where Caxton Hall is, thank you,' Esther replied. 'And I'll certainly consider your invitation. What time tomorrow does this meeting start?'

'Eleven o'clock on the dot. Don't be late, because I'd like you to meet certain people before the meeting actually gets underway. Now, I have to be going, if you'll excuse me. Simon, is it in order with you if we take Esther into our fold?'

'Fine by me,' Simon said with a smile, 'since she seems to have the sort of fire we need to fuel the revolution.'

CHAPTER ELEVEN

'I just think it's a shame that you have to waste our precious Sunday — the only one we've had free together for several weeks — in the company of that bunch of harpies,' Jack complained.

'They're not "harpies",' Esther snapped, bristling. 'Just well-meaning types who're committed to advancing the cause of women throughout the country. They have a point. And let's not lose sight of the fact that we're doing this in order to prove Lucy's innocence.'

'I fail to see how the two are connected,' Jack replied. 'The only link between what happened in Lucy's theatre and this meeting is that one of those attending it is the lover of that pompous blowhard Simon Abelman.'

'We'll just have to see, won't we?' Esther retorted. 'Now, pass me my hat.'

'Why are you going into town with two dead chickens on your head?'

'Because hats like these are the latest fashion, and I want to look the part. Thank God it's not windy out there, so I won't need too many hatpins.'

'Stick one in Simon Abelman with my name on it,' Jack muttered as he grudgingly kissed her goodbye, then stepped out of her way as she headed towards the front door.

The eight-twenty train departed on time, and was not too crowded, given that it was a Sunday morning. When Esther arrived at Euston Station, she was fortunate in being able to board a southbound omnibus that was half empty, and took her down Tottenham Court Road, then Charing Cross Road,

115

all the way to Trafalgar Square. There she alighted and walked across St James's Park to the network of Westminster streets that even at that early hour were busy with tourists, until she finally reached Caxton Hall with a few minutes to spare before the meeting was due to start.

As she entered the rapidly filling hall, Esther caught sight of Florence Bannister waving to her over the top of a myriad of hats whose owners were filing into seats along the serried rows facing the stage. She walked over to where she stood with another woman, a formidable old matron with a fixed, almost painted on, smile.

'Esther, I'd like you to meet Constance Haywood, who's the secretary of our London Branch, which as you can imagine is a fulltime task. She's organised today's meeting, and when the speeches are finished and we adjourn for tea, we'd like you to join us. Now, I've saved us seats down near the front, so let's claim them before somebody else does, shall we?'

The lady to whom Esther had just been introduced made her way down the centre aisle and mounted the steps to the stage, where she began speaking with an elegant, strikingly beautiful woman in her mid-twenties. After a few moments Constance Haywood moved to the front of the stage and clapped her hands for silence. It was doubtful whether the clap could have been heard in even the front row of the audience, given the level of excited chatter, but the gesture was sufficient to reduce several hundred women to total silence, broken only by the rustle of outer clothing. Constance smiled and began to address the audience in a loud voice in order to be heard even at the back.

'I hardly need remind you of the importance of today's meeting, and the qualifications of our main speaker to address it. We've all heard, of course, of the founder of the WSPU,

Mrs Emmeline Pankhurst. Today we welcome her daughter Christabel, who's just returned back amongst us after a dreadful few days in a miserable gaol cell in Manchester, along with her friend and fellow campaigner Annie Kenney. And what did they do to justify such treatment? They had the temerity to attend, as was their right, a public meeting in Manchester, and question the Liberal politician Sir Edward Grey regarding what proposals his party had for promoting the cause of votes for women. That was all, and when he proved evasive on the issue, and Christabel and Annie continued to call for a clear commitment to our cause, they were bundled off and mishandled by half a dozen police bullies, charged with assault and obstruction, and thrown into a cell. It now gives me great pleasure to introduce one of those martyrs to women's rights, who has proposals for where we take our campaign next. Ladies, please welcome Miss Christabel Pankhurst.'

The applause was loud and enthusiastic, mingled with a few shouts that left the main speaker in no doubt that she was among friends. She raised her hands for silence, then addressed the audience in an educated, cultured voice that bore only faint traces of her Manchester origins.

'First of all, friends, thank you for that warm welcome — one that was indeed warmer than the one I received from Sir Edward Grey.' She paused while the polite laughter faded, then continued, 'I think that what Annie and I experienced has clearly shown us the way forward in our campaign to have women granted equal voting rights with men. Those who claim the right to govern our nation have no sensible or honest answers to rational and reasonable questions regarding equality of suffrage between the sexes other than brute force, safe in the knowledge that very few women are equipped to do battle with hulking men armed with billy clubs. But that doesn't mean that we are without weapons of our own.

'Politicians rely on being able to address large rallies in order to promote their cause, and I can see no logical or lawful reason why we can't be allowed the same privilege. "Freedom of speech" is one of our constitutional rights, and we cannot be accused of lawbreaking if we choose to claim it. So I propose that we stage our own rallies, but in such a way as to challenge those who would prefer us to remain silent. Whenever, and wherever, a politician steps up to speak, we should claim the same right, and if our honest and justifiable endeavours have the consequence that the politician cannot get his message across, then at least he'll realise what that feels like, and will become aware of the injustice to which we've been subjected ever since we began our crusade for equal voting rights. Do I hear any disagreement?'

All she heard were shouts of support. She paused until the last of these battle cries had become an echo, then got down to points of detail.

'I suggest that we begin in the larger centres of population in which we have already established branches, including the one here in London managed by my good friend and loyal colleague Constance Haywood. Our Branch Secretaries will keep you all informed of when we plan to disrupt political meetings being held by those who seek to suppress our cause, and will organise the necessary placards, as well as suggest the wording of those demands that we wish to publicise by calling them out in opposition to the platitudes being offered by the official speaker. Hopefully, once the likes of Edward Grey and Winston Churchill begin to realise that freedom of speech works in both directions, we might be invited to present our lawful and reasonable demands in a more civilised atmosphere in which they might even be listened to.'

After another dramatic pause, during which she reached behind her to take a sip of water from the glass on the platform table, she moved on.

'As you have heard, Annie Kenney and I served a few days in dank and unhealthy cells beneath the main police station in Manchester. Some of you are perhaps hesitant to further our cause in the manner I've suggested out of fear of suffering a similar fate. But be heartened by the news that we've begun to recruit lawyers to our cause who are experienced in both criminal and constitutional law, and committed to ensuring that any attempts to thwart our mission by the crude implementation of unlawful tactics will be met with a firm challenge. I hope to graduate in Law myself next year, but of course, being a woman, I won't be allowed to practise. However, it has brought me into contact with men determined to see us take our rightful and equal place in the governance of our society. Be assured that you are not being invited to break the law — simply to employ it to our mutual advantage. So onward and upward, ladies — to a brighter and more equal future!'

'Is your Simon one of those lawyers to whom the speaker was referring?' Esther asked Florence after the meeting had ended. They were drinking tea and nibbling on jam sandwiches alongside Constance Haywood.

Florence nodded enthusiastically over her teacup. 'He is indeed. Not only that, but he's training up others to do the same thing, so that wherever our members are arrested for exercising their lawful rights, they'll be protected from unjust punishment by lawyers who can argue their case. Isn't he *wonderful?*'

'Committed and dedicated, obviously,' Esther conceded. 'But how long before his actions in that regard result in retaliation from the legal establishment? Won't his own professional colleagues seek to silence him, and close down his good work?'

Florence put down her teacup and leaned towards Esther, lowering her voice. 'Simon is very well protected in his work at the highest levels. *Government* levels, that is. It's all very funny, really, when you think about it — one side of the establishment is doing its best to suppress calls for equal suffrage, while the other half is protecting those who're campaigning for it.'

'So when can I sign you up for membership of the London Branch?' Constance asked bluntly.

Esther thought quickly. 'Do you have some sort of paperwork that I can take away with me and read — something containing an address to which I can send a money order?'

'Here,' Constance replied as she reached into a portmanteau at her feet and extracted a few slips of paper held together with pins.

Esther took them with a broad smile. 'Thank you — you'll be hearing from me in due course.' She then made her excuses and wended her way through an almost empty hall and back into the early afternoon streets, eager to share what she'd learned with Jack.

'You presumably aren't here for one of Beattie's cremated breakfasts?' Percy asked as he opened the front door to the Hackney house at shortly before nine o'clock on Monday morning to find Jack on the doorstep. They moved down the hall towards the sitting room. 'But at least stay for a pot of tea while you tell me what you're obviously eager to impart.'

'Is it *so* obvious?' Jack asked.

Percy chuckled. 'Just don't try earning a living at the card table. Now, what do you have to tell me that's inspired you to be late for work at the Yard?'

'Simon Abelman is working with those women who're campaigning for voting rights, and is being protected in high Government places,' Jack announced triumphantly.

'We knew the first part of that already,' Percy reminded him, 'but what do you mean by "high places", exactly?'

'No idea,' Jack admitted. 'It was just something dropped out by his lady friend Florence Bannister while she and Esther were having tea at that meeting that Esther wangled an invitation to. And much though it pains me to say so, perhaps we should be giving Abelman as much attention as we've been giving Ernest Graves.'

Percy sat deep in thought for a moment, then announced, 'I clearly need to meet with Melville again — or "Morgan" as he now calls himself. He may need to know that Abelman is being nursed in his ambitions to save the world by someone high up somewhere. Although, knowing Melville, he's already in possession of that information, and we've been deliberately misled, like ferrets sent down the wrong rabbit hole.'

When Jack looked confused, Percy explained.

'Suppose that Melville's hidden agenda is to protect Abelman, and somehow Graves is threatening to queer his pitch? Perhaps we've been sent to get in Graves's way, and as usual are being manipulated like glove puppets in a side show.'

'Could it also be the other way around?' Jack mused. 'That Abelman's somehow got wind of what Graves is up to, and we were asked to investigate Graves in the hope of discrediting him?'

Percy grimaced. 'Who can tell the way that Melville and his kind operate? But at the very least we need to report back that we know all about Abelman. Perhaps then we'll be given a straight answer about what this is all about. For the time being we regard everyone as a suspect, and let's not lose sight of the fact that we're in this to find out who murdered Primrose, and why. Which reminds me...'

He rose from his chair and walked over to the sideboard, extracting a large buff envelope and taking a portrait-sized photograph from it. 'My good friend Bill Penny worked hard all yesterday, and here's a clear image of the man calling himself "Joe Banks". I suggest that you show it around the Yard, in case anyone knows him by another name. I'll take a copy to Melville in due course, but it won't be today, because Beattie's insisting on my attending a meeting at our local church in the forlorn hope that I can be persuaded to join a committee to assist "fallen women", given my former professional association with East End totties. But don't let that stop you from making your enquiries within the Yard, and perhaps we might provisionally agree to meet at Tang Li's at noon tomorrow, always assuming that I'm allowed to leave my planned meeting with Melville alive.'

Having arrived late for his normal duties at the Yard, Jack went straight to his office with a lame excuse regarding a derailment at Harrow that had delayed his train. Then, when it was time for most of the lower ranks to drift down to what was described as the 'All Ranks' mess room, but rarely saw anyone above the rank of Inspector, he walked there armed with the photograph of Joe Banks, which he pinned to the general noticeboard. Underneath, he added a handwritten request that read: *Anyone with information regarding the identity of this man should lose no time in contacting Chief Inspector Enright.*

His initiative was rewarded the following morning, Tuesday, when he looked up from the paperwork on his desk and saw a uniformed sergeant in his doorway.

'That photograph that you pinned on the noticeboard, sir. I know the bloke, and I'd love to get even with him after he and his lawyer made fools of us.'

'Do come in, and tell me all about it,' Jack replied, smiling invitingly, and his visitor duly obliged, beginning with some personal history of his own.

'I'm Bert Pascoe, sir, currently attached to Recruit Training, as you may know, but until last year I was a sergeant attached to Bow Street, in C Division. If you know the patch, then you'll know that we cover a good bit of the shady end of Covent Garden, with its knocking shops and other grubby operations. There's also a few molly houses in the region of Russell Street, and what you might call "houses of introduction" for those inclined that way. We'd regularly give them a visit and run in anyone we found in them. Anyway, one night towards the end of my time there we turned over this place in Russell Street, and it yielded a couple of blokes who looked decidedly dodgy, so we nicked them.'

'Then what happened?' Jack asked with interest.

'The matter came to trial in front of the magistrates. One bloke — name of "Dark" — was charged with managing a disorderly house, while the other — the bloke in the photograph — was charged with frequenting it. They were both represented by this snooty lawyer who ran rings round us, and made us look like total fools for allegedly "harassing" the lawful owner of a residential dwelling who was being visited by a long-term friend whose mother had recently died, and who was in need of a sympathetic ear. Because we couldn't prove that this was untrue, or that the place was being used for men like them to meet, the case got thrown out, and we got our ears blasted by the superintendent for bringing the service into disrepute. So I'm glad of this opportunity to get my own back — what's the slimy bastard been up to now, sir?'

'I'm not at liberty to say, and perhaps nothing,' Jack replied. 'But "Joe Banks" clearly has a speckled past — we know that.'

'Who's "Joe Banks", sir?' Pascoe asked.

'The man in the photograph,' said Jack. 'Isn't that why you're here?'

'Yes, sir, but that's not his name. I've written down his name on this piece of paper, along with the name of the greasy barrister who got him off. I wouldn't mind a go at him as well, just quietly.'

Jack looked down at the two names, and his eyes opened wide in amazement. 'Thank you, sergeant,' he said with a grin. 'You may well get your wishes fulfilled. Both of them.'

Melville had proved as good as his word, and slightly over an hour after Percy had made the call requesting an appointment, the coach had glided smoothly to a halt outside his business premises. Now here he was, walking through the front door to the house in Tufnell Park Road that seemingly opened of its own accord from the inside.

'In here!' called an imperious voice from within the room that he recalled from his previous visit. He walked in to find Melville seated behind his desk and looking expectant.

'I'd hoped to hear from you earlier than this,' Melville complained.

Percy shrugged. 'I would have been able to report back much quicker had I not been sent down two rabbit holes at the same time,' he grumbled.

'Tea or coffee?' Melville asked, and while a manservant laid out the tea things on the table between them, he went on, 'I'd like to know the reason for your enigmatic response to my observation regarding the delay in reporting back.'

'We're not sure whether you're after Graves or Abelman,' Percy replied. 'You certainly told us to investigate them both, without indicating any possible connection between them, but both of them seem to operate behind a Government protection barrier. Or so Abelman's given to boasting.'

'Dispense with the sleight of mouth, Percy, and tell me what you're getting at,' Melville said impatiently.

Percy took a deep breath. 'First of all, Graves, regarding whom I can report nothing except the fact that he may — and I emphasise *may* — have had a hand in ensuring that the fatal knife was in the hands of Leopold Carter. But for that I'm relying on the possibly polluted memory of a stagehand whose loyalties could be a little suspect, given her emotional attachment to another stagehand who was well placed to organise for the knife to be sabotaged. He's called Joe Banks — at least, that's the name he's using, but it's probably as false as the life story he's concocted of being the doting son of an elderly mother with whom he resides in Bethnal Green. He prefers the company of men; I followed him to a molly house that probably costs a fortune to belong to, and that makes one more man of that persuasion to add to the collection. The deceased actor, Primrose, was a practising homosexual who actually shared living accommodation with Leopold Carter, so that threw an additional squib into the fire when it came to possible motivation.'

'So why were you going on about Abelman?'

'Because he's committed himself to this revolutionary female outfit who're trying to get votes for women, and claims to enjoy the protection of high-ranking Government officials. The only remaining question in my mind is whether you're the one pulling the diversionary string, or whether someone's sent *you* barking up the wrong tree.'

'You're making even less sense than usual,' Melville complained, 'and it's probably in order for me to request that Kell joins us, in the hope that he knows what you're drivelling on about.'

He picked up a telephone on his desk and made the necessary request. In less than two minutes Kell had joined them, and was demanding answers.

'I'm obviously more concerned about what Graves has been up to,' he reminded Percy, 'and I'll leave anything to do with Abelman for Melville to worry about. What have you learned about Graves?'

'Almost nothing,' Percy told him, 'except that he *may* have been in a position to place the murder weapon into innocent hands. But I was hoping that between you, the two of you might cast further light on a shadowy character calling himself Joe Banks. He's working as a stagehand in the theatre in which Primrose was murdered, and he's not what he pretends to be. Since the world that you two occupy is full of people like that, I was hoping that you could identify him, since he could be the real villain behind all this.'

'What did you say his assumed name was — "Banks"?' Kell asked. 'Can't say that the name rings a bell.'

'I have his photograph here, if it helps,' Percy offered, as he extracted the image of Banks and handed it across to Kell, who started visibly.

'How did you get this?' he asked.

'By my usual stealth,' said Percy. 'Do you know him?'

'You could say that,' Kell replied, ashen-faced. 'That's Mark Adlington.'

CHAPTER TWELVE

'I know who Joe Banks really is!' Jack blurted excitedly before Percy had even taken the vacant seat at their usual corner table in Tang Li's.

'So do I,' Percy replied as he sat down, 'and his real name is Mark Adlington. I can also tell you how he fits into the jigsaw we've been asked to solve.'

'How did you learn that?' Jack asked dejectedly.

'From Melville, or "Morgan", as he's still calling himself, although it was Kell who made the actual identification from the photograph I showed him. And Adlington works alongside Graves in Naval Intelligence, holding the keys to the vault that was once opened to allow Graves to send plans of our latest warship to the Germans.'

'But at the theatre, Graves and Banks — sorry, "Adlington" — never give any indication that they know each other outside of their drama connection.'

'Well, they wouldn't, would they? Now, are you having meat pie or something else? I can see the waiter hovering, and in just a moment he'll descend upon us with his notepad.'

'I was going to have chicken chow mien, but you've killed my appetite, so probably meat pie. But there *is* something else I can tell you, which probably not even Melville was aware of.'

'Go on, amaze me,' said Percy, raising an eyebrow.

'Adlington was once arrested for being caught in a house that was being used for meetings of homosexual men, but he managed to get himself acquitted. Or rather, his barrister did. Guess who?'

'Abelman?'

'There's really no surprising you, is there?' Jack complained. 'How did you guess?'

'How many barristers are we currently investigating, and how many would you have been likely to recognise by name? It was a simple exercise in logic. Yes, we'll both have the meat pie,' he told the waiter, then smiled sympathetically back at Jack. 'Don't look so despondent, since what you've discovered gives us another line of enquiry to pursue, namely that Adlington — and let's keep calling him "Banks", shall we? — may have been working in league with Abelman.'

'His most obvious master would surely be Graves?' Jack suggested. 'And that girl Alice Bennett heard Graves — or it *could* have been Abelman — with Carter just before they went on stage, urging him to pick up the knife and join the others before the curtain opened for the assassination scene.'

'So we're back to the same two who Melville and Kell wanted us to investigate in the first place,' Percy observed thoughtfully. 'But now we know that they *both* had links with Banks, and reasons why he might feel obliged to do their bidding. Interestingly enough, I got the impression that neither Melville nor Kell knew of any connection between Abelman and Banks. Or if they did, they were keeping very silent about it. And something else has been bothering me for a week or two now. Ask yourself why Lucy hasn't yet been arrested.'

'Because she's innocent?'

'We know that, but if you were Inspector Buxton, wouldn't you have charged her by now, on the evidence you had?'

'Probably, but what's your point?'

'My point is that I'm beginning to smell a rat where Melville and Kell are concerned. I think we've been sent down two rabbit holes at once in an attempt to obscure the one they're really interested in, which may lead to why Primrose was murdered in the first place. It's obviously in their interest to prevent Lucy from being arrested just yet — enough to keep urging us forward.'

'So you think that Melville and Kell are leaning on Buxton to hold back from arresting Lucy?'

'More likely Melville, but yes. And in one sense we should be grateful for that. But I don't like being used as a puppet.' Percy frowned. 'Jack, I want you to break your cover so far as that Alice Bennett's concerned.'

'Why? She's our best source of information at this stage,' Jack argued.

'And she might be likely to give you even more if you reveal why you're really pretending to be an actor, and why Esther's playing at being a stage manager. Particularly if you let her believe that you might otherwise suspect her.'

'That would be a dreadful lie, and I'm not sure the poor girl could survive such a terrible accusation.'

'You can withdraw it in exchange for her disclosing everything she knows, particularly with regard to who had access to that props cupboard.'

'I still think it would be unethical,' Jack objected.

Percy let out a hollow laugh. 'Have you learned nothing from me after all these years? In my book, "ethics" is the county to the north-east of London in which you were raised. And me, for that matter.'

Jack shook his head. 'How do you propose that I go about it? And do you have any bright ideas about how I might sell the idea to Esther?'

'The second issue is for you to determine, and as for the first, I've already told you — make her think she's a suspect herself.'

*

'I don't like the idea one little bit,' Esther protested when Jack put it to her on Tuesday evening on his return from the Yard, having already decided that he wouldn't be attending a line rehearsal in which he wasn't required. 'The poor girl's totally innocent.'

'We don't know that,' Jack countered, 'and for all we know, Banks — or "Adlington", to give him his correct name — seduced her into becoming involved.'

'Use the evidence of your eyes, Jack,' said Esther. 'She wouldn't still be hanging around him like a lovesick puppy if he'd already seduced her.'

'She might,' said Jack. 'First he shows her what might be called "the promised land", then goes all cold again until the next time he needs to use her. It's a common practice.'

'I won't enquire too closely into how you know that,' said Esther, glowering, 'but I don't believe that's what happened with Alice. She's a bit dull, certainly, and lacking in what you might call a smart brain, which makes her open to exploitation, but that just underlines her innocence. To openly accuse her of being complicit in the murder of Primrose would be a terrible blow to her, given her already low self-esteem.'

'I voiced similar reservations to Percy, but he seemed to think that the ends would justify the means, to quote a phrase that he often employs. Something to do with an Italian villain, I believe.'

'So do we have a choice?' Esther asked reluctantly. 'And if not, how do you propose that we set about it?'

'I was giving it some thought on the train coming home,' Jack replied, 'and you seem to have developed a friendly relationship with her. So why not invite her to take tea with you after Saturday's rehearsal, and by a happy coincidence I'll be sitting waiting for you both?'

'Do you know anywhere near there that will be likely to be open on a Saturday afternoon?'

'Not offhand,' Jack admitted, 'but we can always ask Lucy, since she lives in the area, and is always aware of the latest social trends. Leave that to me.'

'I'll have to, since I'm up to my armpits in administration at the school, now that Emily's out of the running,' Esther admitted. 'I've got prospective parents scheduled for a guided tour of the place tomorrow, and Doris and I need to start work on our end-of-school-year reports.'

'It's nowhere near the end of the school year yet, is it?'

'It's closer than you'd think. Besides, we don't just sit down and write them all at the last minute. We have to have them all ready for the pupils to take home with them on their final day.'

'Well, at least you won't need to write any for Lily and Annabelle,' said Jack.

Esther chuckled, 'You think not? Aunt Beattie was insistent on getting one for Annabelle.'

'How is Annabelle doing, anyway?'

'Very well indeed,' said Esther, smiling. 'There are only five currently in the senior class, including Annabelle, and she's head and shoulders above the rest of them, particularly when it comes to English and artistic expression. She's currently pestering me to let her write a play for performance by Lucy's theatre group.'

'We might let her write one about the murder on stage of an actor playing the part of Julius Caesar,' said Jack with a laugh, and Esther smacked him playfully across the hand.

'Don't even joke about that, and don't forget to ask Lucy where we can take poor Alice in order to frighten the life out of her.'

*

132

The Saturday stage rehearsal was basically a repeat, and a refinement, of the previous Saturday's walk-through of Act One. Jack proved himself line-perfect yet again, earning lavish praise from Lucy and resentful stares from Simon, Ernest and Henry. He was, in fact, so comfortable now with what he was achieving that he had time to surreptitiously watch Joe Banks for any sign of familiarity with either Ermest or Simon, but whatever secrets they were hiding were being held close to their chests.

There was the usual break for lunch, when Jack took the opportunity to request that he be allowed to leave the afternoon rehearsal early in order to keep a personal appointment, and shortly after three o'clock he made his farewells. Esther was busily completing the last of the sewing work that had been dumped on her, and Alice was busy clearing away the remains of their lunch and ensuring that the kitchen was clean and tidy. When she was almost finished, Esther called through the kitchen door from where she was seated at the table in the dressing room, 'Alice, would you like to meet my husband?'

Alice poked her head around the door and asked, 'Why would I want to do that?'

'Well,' Esther explained, 'it's more the case that I'd like to get to know you better. After all, we're working together on this latest production, and our paths seem destined to cross all the time. My husband's taking me to afternoon tea in a local hotel that opens on Saturday afternoons, and it would be a perfect opportunity for him to meet one of the people I'm working with here, and for you to meet the man I married four children ago. Of course, if you'd rather not, I understand.'

'No, that would be nice,' said Alice, smiling. 'It's just that I'm not blessed with much in the way of spare money after I've paid for my room rent, and all the other things I need.'

'Please don't worry about that,' Esther insisted. 'We're very fortunate that my husband has a successful career, and you'd be attending as our guest.'

'In that case, I'd be delighted,' Alice replied, beaming, 'and the sooner I get this kitchen back to a normal level of cleanliness, the sooner I can accept your very kind invitation.'

The actors were still arguing among themselves, and with Lucy, regarding certain aspects of the stage directions that she'd been insisting on, when Esther and Alice wished them a good afternoon and slipped away. They walked down several side streets that took them on to the broad thoroughfare known as Holborn Kingsway, halfway down which was located the popular and well patronised Holborn Restaurant.

'I do hope my husband managed to reserve us a seat,' Esther said as they picked their way through dozens of tables, dodging smartly dressed waitresses who were passing to and fro with plates of sandwiches, tiers of fancy cakes and pots of tea on silver salvers. Then she gave a happy cry.

'There he is — over on that side wall. Do come and be introduced!'

Alice was a few paces behind Esther as they approached the table at which Jack sat with a broad smile behind a platter of sandwiches and a stack of fancy cakes, drinking tea. As he rose to welcome them, indicating that they should take the two spare seats, Alice stopped dead in her tracks and spluttered, 'But that's Jack! I thought we were meeting your husband.'

'Then allow me to introduce him,' said Esther as she took Alice gently by the sleeve of her coat and guided her to the seat on Jack's left. 'His name really *is* Jack, but his second name is "Enright". So is mine.'

'But I thought you were Lucy's sister-in-law,' Alice objected.

Esther lowered herself into the spare seat on Jack's right and confirmed, 'So I am, but not married to her brother-in-law. Instead, I'm married to her brother. Lucy is Jack's younger sister.'

'But why the pretence?' Alice asked, utterly bewildered by what was being revealed.

This time it was Jack who offered the explanation. 'We needed to preserve our anonymity in order to investigate the murder of Valentine Primrose, primarily to ensure that Lucy wasn't charged with it by that dreadful Inspector Buxton.'

'But he *is* a police officer, after all,' Alice pointed out.

'So am I, and at a rank higher than his,' said Jack. 'I'm a *Chief* Inspector inside Scotland Yard.'

Alice seemed to have run out of things to say, so Esther filled the silence.

'If people at the theatre knew who Jack really was, they'd be on their guard, and we wouldn't be able to learn anything regarding what really happened. Someone among the cast of *Julius Caesar* murdered Val Primrose, but it wasn't Lucy, of that we're sure.'

'Then who do you suspect?' Alice asked, as Jack held out the sandwich platter.

'The salmon ones are very tasty. Do please help yourself,' he said.

Alice took a sandwich and placed it on the small plate in front of her as Esther explained, 'Somebody obviously interfered in advance with one of those knives, and we need to find out who that was.'

'But they would have needed access to the props cupboard, and apart from Lucy you were the only other person with a key to it,' Jack added as he stared hard into her eyes.

She seemed to wilt, then dropped the sandwich back onto the plate and protested, 'It wasn't me! Please, you have to believe me, it wasn't me!'

'But if it wasn't Lucy, and you had the only other key…' Jack repeated, allowing the implication to hang in the air.

'Unless you loaned it to someone,' Esther prompted her.

Alice nodded eagerly. 'I did! Quite a lot, actually, because he often needed to go in there for props.'

'Who's he?' Jack asked.

'Joe, of course. But I'd trust him with my life. In fact, well — that is…'

'It's quite obvious, to me, anyway, that you have a soft spot for Joe,' Esther told her gently, 'but Jack knows something about him that he needs to tell you.'

Alice looked helplessly at Jack and asked, 'What? Is he secretly married or something?'

'No, he's not,' Jack told her, 'and not likely to be in the future. The fact is that — well, to put it as delicately as I can, he's not interested in women.'

'He certainly doesn't seem to be interested in me,' Alice replied with a shake of her head, 'despite all my efforts to engage his attention.'

'It's not just you, Alice,' Esther added as she placed a consoling hand on her sleeve, 'it's women in general.'

'You mean he's — that is, he — well, you hear about those sorts of people, I know, but I've never met one before, as far as I know.'

'You have now,' Jack confirmed, 'and let's not mince words, Alice. Joe is what they call a "homosexual". And his real name isn't "Joe", either.'

'But how do you know these things?' Alice persisted.

'I've been making my own enquiries, and someone working for me followed him to a club in Soho that exists just for people like him,' Jack told her. 'And he doesn't have a sick mother living in Bethnal Green, either — that's just a story he made up.'

'But why?' Alice demanded. 'Why did he need to make up stories about his background? And what's his real reason for being a member of the theatre club?'

'We were rather hoping that you could help us answer that question,' Esther replied. 'Once you've got over the shock, of course.'

Alice sat there in silence for what seemed like an eternity, and Jack and Esther were exchanging concerned glances in case they'd gone too far too quickly. Then Alice suddenly spoke.

'To think how I made such a fool of myself, trying to make myself amenable, even attractive, to *him*. All I wanted was a young man of my own, someone who'd take me for walks and hold my hand, then maybe one day ask me to marry him and have his babies. I feel so *stupid*! What must you think of me?'

Tears welled in her eyes, and Esther nodded to Jack, who reached over and put his arm around her shoulder.

'What *I* think is that if I hadn't met and married Esther when I did, I'd have been looking for a girl just like you. Warm, generous of heart, hardworking, loyal and pleasant on the eye. But Esther's all of those things as well, and she got in first.'

Alice chuckled despite herself, then leaned forward and kissed Jack on the cheek. 'You're *so* lovely!' she murmured. 'And Esther's *so* lucky.'

'She's also a bit peckish,' Esther said with a grin, 'so race you to the last salmon sandwich. Then we can start on the ham and watercress ones.'

They were into the second layer of cakes before Alice broke her silence a second time.

'If Lucy didn't interfere with that knife, and I know I didn't, then it *must* have been Joe, mustn't it?'

'But what reason would Joe have for wanting Valentine Primrose dead?' Jack asked. 'Did they have an enmity going back a long time?'

'Not so far as I know,' Alice replied. 'In fact, Joe hasn't been in our theatre group for very long. He arrived just as we were starting rehearsals for *Julius Caesar*, and at first I was a bit resentful, because it meant that I wasn't the only one doing stage management.'

'What reason did he give for joining?' said Jack.

Alice shrugged. 'He didn't. It was Ernie Graves who did all the talking for him. He said that Joe was a poorly paid clerk in his place of work, and needed some extra money in order to help his sick and widowed mother.'

'One time before, when we were talking in the theatre,' Esther reminded her, 'you told me that you heard Graves, or it could have been Abelman, arguing with Carter over the final two knives before they went on stage for the assassination scene. Could you tell us more about that?'

'Not really,' Alice admitted. 'And it wasn't about the knives as such, just that Leo needed to get on stage quickly. I'm not even sure who it was who was yelling at him — it could have been either Ernie or Simon.'

'You also told Esther that when you went into the dressing room immediately afterwards, there was an extra knife on the table,' said Jack. 'Can you tell us any more about that?'

'It was odd, certainly,' Alice confirmed, 'since all the actors were on stage by then, waiting for the curtain to go up for the assassination scene. I was in two minds over whether or not to rush into the wings and ask if someone had forgotten their knife, but then I heard the curtains go up, and Caesar delivering the opening line, which was "The ides of March are come". So I just put the spare knife back in the props cupboard.'

'You had the key to it at that point?' Jack asked.

Alice nodded. 'I actually counted, just to make sure, and the one I put back made it three left in the cupboard.'

'But if there were eight to begin with, as Lucy told us,' said Esther, calculating quickly, 'and three left in the cupboard, with five on stage, then one of the original eight must have been interfered with in advance. Or have I got that wrong?'

'No, that would be right,' Alice agreed, 'and I've just remembered something else. It can't have been Simon who was arguing with Leo, because he'd already gone on stage ready for the curtain to go up, taking the others with him. I remember because he made one of his loud, dramatic announcements — something along the lines of "Very well, gentlemen — we have a bloody death to bring about. Let's go to it!" Or something like that, anyway.'

'You mentioned the curtains opening for the start of the assassination scene,' Esther reminded her. 'Who would have been opening the curtain, and how is it done on nights when you have an audience?'

'There's a pulley system operated from the "stage left" wings,' Alice explained. 'They're the ones on the same side as the exit from the dressing room, and the actors would have passed Joe as he was waiting to open the curtains. It's organised that way so that the person on the curtains can be sure that everyone's in position before working the pulley, and can nip back to the dressing room in order to hasten them along if need be.'

'So could it have been Joe who was urging Carter to get on stage?' Jack asked.

Alice shook her head. 'No, I'd definitely have recognised his voice. I'm almost certain that it was either Ernest or Simon, and most likely Ernest, for the reasons that I've already given you.'

'And you've been a great help to us,' Jack said with a smile. 'Rest assured that we don't for one moment suspect you, but we'd be grateful if you'd keep our little secret. And if possible, don't let Joe know that you've been advised of his true nature.'

'I'll certainly keep your secret, and thank you so much for the afternoon tea,' Alice replied. 'As for Joe, I just want to smack him across the face.'

'We'd rather you didn't,' Esther said with a laugh.

Alice took her leave of them, and as Jack paid the bill Esther reached across and kissed him warmly on the lips.

'You almost brought me to tears when you were so sweet to poor Alice. You can be *so* gallant when it suits your purpose.'

'*Our* purpose,' Jack reminded her. 'Which is to prove Lucy's innocence by identifying the real killer. And what Alice can tell us may well be the key to doing that.'

CHAPTER THIRTEEN

'You only just caught me,' Percy frowned as he answered Jack's knock on his front door. 'I was on my way to the estate agents, who ought, by rights, to have put Primrose's former apartment on the market, but haven't done so yet. Anyway, come in, have a cup of tea, and tell me what brings you to my door at nine o'clock on a Monday morning. How did Alice take the glad tidings about the object of her affections preferring the company of men? I assume that you told her?'

'Indeed we did, and it came as quite a shock to her, as you can imagine. But when she finally accepted that Joe Banks, or Mark Adlington, was not destined to be the father of her children, she disclosed that he only joined the theatre group when they started rehearsing for "Julius Caesar", and that he was introduced into it by Ernest Graves.'

'That merely confirms what we suspected,' Percy replied. 'Did she give you any more information about the events of the fatal night?'

'Only to confirm that it was almost certainly either Abelman or Graves who arranged for Carter to take the knife that had been interfered with. But she said that Abelman was already on stage by that point, and that a spare knife was still lying on the table in the dressing room after all the actors had taken theirs in. How could that be?'

'Did she put the spare back in the cupboard, and did she by any chance recall how many were already still in there?'

'Yes — she's certain that when she put the spare one back that made it three in the cupboard. Add in the five on stage, and that accounts for all eight of them. That surely means that someone gained access in advance to the knife that was doctored?'

'It certainly seems that way,' Percy agreed. 'Did she give you anything of value regarding who might have had access to the props cupboard?'

'She confirmed that Joe Banks regularly borrowed her key to access props, but again I think we already guessed that.'

'Did she agree to work with us in future?'

'Yes, she's happy to assist Esther and I in future.'

'That's good, because what we need to know next is who could have stolen Lucy's hatpin.'

'Again, that could have been anybody. Alice could hardly be expected to have witnessed what would have been a fleeting moment of theft.'

'All the same,' Percy insisted, 'any glimmer of light that she can cast on that will lead us to the killer. Why else would they have stolen a hatpin?'

'If you say so, but at least we can now concentrate more on Graves.'

'You think so?' Percy challenged him. 'Our instruction was to spy on Abelman as well, remember, and I for one am not prepared to rule him out unless and until we can firmly point the finger at Graves. Is Esther following up on her contact with that Florence woman?'

'Florence Bannister? Yes, I suppose so, although it's gone very quiet on that front since she attended that meeting the previous week.'

'Well, tell her to keep in touch with that side of things. And you must both now double your efforts to detect possible ongoing connections between Banks, Graves and Abelman.'

'That's not so simple when we're all on stage every Saturday, being positioned by Lucy, like Bertie arranging his toy soldiers.'

'What about the other meetings? Aren't there rehearsals on Tuesday and Thursday evenings?'

'Yes, but they're just what they call "line rehearsals", when the actors sit in a circle and read their lines from the script. Esther doesn't have a part in the play, and my character doesn't come into Act Two at all — that's the part of the play they're currently working on.'

'That won't do.' Percy frowned. 'We need you to be at that theatre on every feasible occasion, in order to watch carefully and get what further information you can from that Alice woman, who you must now regard as one of the team. You should also watch carefully for any change in the attitude of the remaining theatre members towards you and Esther, in case Alice has revealed your secret, innocently or otherwise.'

'I'll try and think of something,' Jack promised, 'but now I'd better get down to the Yard with some flabby excuse for my lateness, such as another derailment.'

The old harridan with the winged spectacles frowned as Percy pushed open the door to 'Regency Properties' and walked towards her counter.

'I remember you,' she announced coldly. 'You're from some rival property company, and you want to purchase one of the properties that we manage.'

'Well remembered,' Percy said in what he hoped was a flattering tone. 'To be precise, my name is Percival, and I'm from Crown Properties. I have a client who wants to purchase Apartment Two in Addlebrook Mansions in Green Street, and he won't take "no" for an answer. He's appallingly rich, and very determined.'

'I don't care how rich, or how determined he is,' the lady replied, scowling. 'The property isn't for sale.'

'So the owner has decided to use it as a source of income from rentals, rather than sell it outright for enough money to secure his financial future, is that it?'

'None of your business,' the lady replied. 'Now, if you'll excuse me, I have work to do.'

'So do I,' Percy told her, 'and it involves finding out why a property as valuable as that is still not for sale. And I have my methods. Good day to you, madam.'

'I'm not sure we're going to get away with this,' Esther warned Jack as he met her off the early evening train at Euston, 'and I really have so many better things to do with my time now that I'm running a school.'

'Better than proving Lucy's innocence?' Jack challenged her.

She shook her head. 'Obviously not better than that, but I really can't imagine that the other members will believe that we're so desperate to advance our careers as actors that we're prepared to give up two evenings a week to read parts that aren't ours in the first place.'

'I couldn't think of any better excuse,' Jack admitted, 'and Percy was insistent. He has a point. We need to keep in regular contact with Alice, and take every chance we can get to find out who stole that hatpin. The rehearsals tend to be somewhat unrealistic, with Lucy reading all the minor parts for which she's going to have to borrow actors from other theatre groups. We should be quite convincing as eager outsiders who're seizing a chance to prove that we're capable of being considered ourselves.'

'Even so,' Esther objected, 'can you *really* see me as Ophelia?'

'I did once, when I auditioned for Laertes,' Jack reminded her with a smile, but she just pouted.

'It's all very well for you, because you'll just be reading for a servant's part. What was his name again — "Raymondo" or something?'

'Reynaldo, servant to Polonius, which will of course bring me closer to Graves. And if we're hopeless at it, that'll just enhance our assumed roles as hopeful actors with limited talent.'

'If you say so, but I hope we don't inadvertently reveal our false identities,' said Esther. 'I really hate pretending that I'm somebody I'm not.'

'Well, this evening pretend that you're Ophelia,' said Jack with a grin as they walked out into the forecourt and hailed a cab.

'Arriving together, I see,' Simon remarked suggestively as Esther and Jack appeared in the communal dressing room, where most of the company had already gathered. 'Do I detect a budding romance?'

'We're both respectable and happily married people,' Esther replied, bristling, 'and we happened to meet up in the doorway downstairs.'

'All the same,' Simon persisted, 'neither of you is really required for a Tuesday evening line rehearsal.'

'I thought I'd assist by reading the parts for which Lucy will be borrowing actors from other companies,' Jack explained, trying his best to look sheepish. 'I mentioned that possibility to Esther on Saturday, and she thought she might do the same with Ophelia.'

'Good luck with that, sweetheart,' Simon muttered. 'Not even Lucy's prepared to take that on, but give it a try, anyway.'

They were halfway through the line reading of Act Two, Scene One, when the door from the corridor opened hurriedly, and in blustered Leopold Carter, his script under his arm and contrition written across his face.

'My sincere apologies for the late arrival,' he said breathlessly, 'but I've just received some rather unsettling news. I'm required to leave my current accommodation by the end of the month.'

'Been a naughty boy, have we?' Simon prodded.

Before Leopold could reply, Lucy said, 'Take a seat, Leo, and just ignore Simon. As it turns out you didn't hold us back, since Horatio doesn't come in until the second scene, and we were just about to start on that. So let's get back into it, shall we?'

When the rehearsal ended, and the company took itself off to the Lamb and Flag, Jack made a point of not walking alongside Esther. Since neither Joe nor Alice had attended the rehearsal, he sidled up to Ernest Graves and asked how he was enjoying playing the part of Polonius.

'A bit of a challenge, playing an old man,' Ernest replied, 'but it adds to my repertoire, and if you have ambitions to earn your living on the stage, then flexibility is essential. I thought you did pretty well as my servant, by the way.'

'Thank you,' Jack replied, 'but of course it's not as challenging as playing Laertes.'

'You're damned good in that part as well,' Ernest complimented him, 'and I was hoping that Lucy might give Reynaldo's part to Joe in due course. The poor lad really does need something to uplift him, what with the responsibility of a sick mother and all that.'

'I gather that you two work together,' Jack commented casually.

Ernest frowned. 'Who told you that?' he demanded.

Jack did his best to look confused. 'I can't remember, to be honest. Probably Alice, while we were having lunch last Saturday, or maybe the Saturday before. She's got quite a sweet spot for Joe, I think, and I was wondering if their absence from this evening's rehearsal was because they'd made plans of their own, if you get my drift.'

'I think you'll find that Joe's not really attracted to Alice, if you had a mind to try your luck there,' Ernest replied matter-of-factly. 'Although, as Simon rudely observed during your grand entrance together, perhaps your stronger interest is in Esther.'

'As Esther herself pointed out,' Jack replied coldly, 'we're both happily married.' He opted to leave it at that, and dropped back slightly so that he was the last to enter the pub.

When he did so, he noticed Esther talking intently with Simon Abelman, and made a point of sitting across from them in an attempt to lipread their conversation. But the background noise was distracting, and Simon kept moving his head from side to side, so he gave up, knowing that Esther would report the conversation when they got home.

'You made a pretty decent stab at Ophelia,' Simon flattered Esther. 'Were you perhaps hoping to snare the part?'

'Not really,' Esther replied with an air of assumed modesty. 'It's a leading part, and I'm only just starting on the road to being an actress. Or so I hope, anyway.'

'I've told you before,' Simon replied as he laid his hand on the sleeve of her costume jacket, 'you should never hide your light under a bushel, and more to the point you should be pushing hard to show that women are more than capable of running the world. What did you think of the meeting that Flo took you to?'

'Very interesting, and very uplifting, in a way,' Esther replied. 'At least I now know that there are many other women like myself, struggling for acceptance and recognition.'

'Would you be interested in pursuing your association with the WSPU to the next stage?'

'Yes, I think so,' Esther replied. 'I've got membership forms ready to fill in, and I'll be posting them off, probably tomorrow.'

'I can save you the cost of a stamp,' said Simon, smiling. 'After the rehearsal on Thursday you can accompany me to another pub, rather than drag along behind this dreary mob. It's called the Welsh Harp, and it's just down the road in Covent Garden. Flo and a few others will be there, discussing another meeting on Sunday of this week, so why don't you come along and join us? You can bring your completed membership form along with you.'

'I'd like that,' Esther replied graciously, 'and thank you for the invitation. Now, I'd better be leaving, before my husband thinks that I've run away with the circus or something.'

'I thought you'd like to know that Carter's been given his marching orders from that apartment he was living in with Primrose,' Jack told Percy over the telephone the following morning, 'and Esther's lined up another meeting with Abelman's little coven of determined ladies.'

'Very interesting,' Percy observed, 'because the property company that I visited only yesterday claims that the apartment in which Primrose was living won't be going on the market. I'd be very interested to learn who their client is, since whoever's sitting on that valuable asset clearly doesn't need the money, and may well be connected with a highly placed group of men who for some reason or other wanted Primrose dead.'

'And knowing you, you'll make it your business to find out?'

'You know me so well, Jack. Wish me luck.'

Every day for the next week a beggar sat on the pavement, propped up against the front wall of a business block in Green Street, Mayfair, which housed lawyers, opticians, dentists and a shipping agency, and was conveniently located across the road from Addlebrook Mansions. His face was all but obscured by a beard that was not his own, and one arm of his heavily stained army greatcoat hung lifeless at his side as he occasionally called out to passing pedestrians in order to reinforce the crudely scrawled message behind his collecting hat that denoted him as 'War Wounded' and appealed for generous donations.

On the fifth day he was rewarded by the sight of a coach pulling up across the road, and a man emerging from the front entrance to the mansion block, hauling several bags that the coachman hastily dismounted in order to assist him with. Percy knew Leopold Carter by sight, having recently taken his photograph while wearing a different disguise. It was obvious that Jack's information had been accurate, and that Carter was moving residence.

Two days later, a nattily dressed individual sporting a goatee beard stepped down from a coach that pulled up in front of the apartment block and began ordering the coachman and his lad to unload boxes, bags and a small crate that they carried into Addlebrook Mansions. The man was unfamiliar to Percy, but there was every reason to believe that he was the new tenant of the premises that had until several weeks ago been the town residence of the late Valentine Primrose. Percy would be very interested to learn who the landlords were — the ones whose identities were being loyally guarded by the property agents. If there was a ring of rich men who preferred male company living a secret life in one of the wealthiest areas of London, then someone might have been very keen to silence Valentine, and there were several men of like persuasion who were members of Lucy's theatre group.

There was one way to gain more information, and one with which Percy was more than familiar. Changing his appearance to one of a blind beggar selling matches from a tray — which he'd purchased from just such a man several streets away — he positioned himself outside the apartment block early one morning and waited for the bearded man to exit and hail a passing cab. Then Percy walked up the stairs to the second floor and used his skeleton keys to enter.

It didn't take him long to realise that the apartment was still largely furnished in the same classical style that it had been during Valentine's tenancy. The statuettes were still there, and the mock Greek columns, but the clothing hanging in the main wardrobe was clearly that of the man who'd left earlier. Percy set about learning what he could about its new tenant. Despite rummaging through drawers and cupboards, he could acquire no clue as to who that might be, or the identity of his landlords, and he gave up the search and opted for a swift departure.

As he silently re-opened the front door, he became instantly aware of two burly police constables standing in the hallway with raised billy clubs, clearly awaiting his departure.

'Got yer, yer sneaky bastard!' one of them announced triumphantly. 'An' not yer first time, neither, accordin' ter the neighbour what called us. Put yer arms up yer back, else I'll pull 'em up there fer yer, an' I won't be ser gentle about it.'

'You should know that I used to be a detective inspector at the Yard,' Percy announced, to two derisive snorts from the constables.

'Yeah, right, an' I used ter be Queen Victoria's ballet teacher,' one of them replied. 'Arms up yer back — nah!'

CHAPTER FOURTEEN

'So glad you could join us,' Florence Bannister beamed as Simon Abelman led Esther into the private room at the rear of the Welsh Harp, where she recognised one or two other faces from the meeting she'd attended in Caxton Hall. One of them belonged to Constance Haywood, who'd been introduced to Esther on that occasion as the Secretary of the London Branch of the WSPU. Esther handed over her completed membership form, containing entirely fictitious details, along with a money order for thirty shillings. Constance thanked her, then placed the documentation in a bulky portmanteau.

Simon asked Esther what she'd like to drink, and she settled for a small gin and tonic. He chuckled as he reminded her, 'They call it "mother's ruin" in some circles, but not this one. Anyway, I'll shut up and let Connie do the talking.'

Constance Haywood looked individually at each of the eight or so individuals seated around the table before advising them, 'Christabel wants us to turn up the pressure, and she suggests that we assemble outside Caxton Hall next Wednesday afternoon, and march on Parliament House. I have enough contacts to ensure that there'll be at least fifty of us, but if any of you know of others who'd like to shout in favour of increased rights for women — not just with the vote, but in lots of other ways — then feel free to bring them along. We'll make as much noise as we can while the House of Commons is in its afternoon session, and I'll make sure that the newspapers are fully alerted.'

'Won't we be at risk of being arrested for breach of the peace or something?' a nervous woman three seats away from Esther asked, but Constance shook her head.

'For one thing, Simon will be there to ensure that anyone charged with that will be fully represented in front of the magistrate, and that they'll be acquitted on the grounds that they were simply exercising their constitutional right to free speech. And in any case, there's normally only a token guard of half a dozen or so bobbies on duty at the doors of Parliament House, and a hundred women or so will be more than equal to them. They might formally arrest a couple of us, but as I say Simon will get them off, and we'll have made our point. But we hope that the newspapers will pick up our message, which will be all over the following day's front pages.'

'I still think it'll be risky,' the doubter muttered.

Constance glared in her direction. '*Everything* we do is risky, Millie — you knew that before you joined. We've tried the usual channels of diplomacy, asked to meet with leading politicians, even heckled their public meetings, but only in small, meek numbers. Once they realise that we can be counted in our hundreds, possibly thousands, and that we don't intend to be silenced, perhaps they'll bring the issue of women's suffrage higher up their precious agenda. That's what Christabel thinks, anyway, and she has more experience in these matters than the rest of us put together. So I take it that we're all game?'

There were nods and murmurs of agreement all round, and Constance thanked them all for attending, then confirmed the meeting time and place. 'But only *outside* Caxton Hall, remember, not inside. It's a convenient meeting point for a march on Parliament House, which is only a half a mile or so down the road from there.'

'You'll be attending, I take it?' Simon asked of Esther, who nodded with feigned enthusiasm.

'Of course! I think I've been waiting for years to make my voice heard, and thank you *so* much to you and Florence for giving me the opportunity. We have a nanny for the children, so getting away during the day won't be a problem for me.'

'That's agreed, then,' Simon said with a smile. 'And I'll see you at rehearsals before then, of course. May I say what a superb job you're doing, sitting in as Ophelia? You really should be pushing to actually play the part.'

'That's very kind of you,' Esther replied, trying to make herself blush. Simon had no idea just *how* good she was at pretending to be someone she wasn't.

She got back home late and discovered that Jack had already retired to bed, and was snoring gently as she tiptoed into their bedroom. She therefore kept her news until the following morning, when she told Jack over their toast and eggs what was planned for the following Wednesday.

'You'd better let Percy know about it,' Jack told her. 'I assume that you have no intention of actually attending yourself, to be bundled into the back of a wagon by a couple of beefy-handed bobbies?'

'What do *you* think? Of course I won't, but I'll need a good excuse for not turning up.'

'Perhaps we'll get Percy to think one up for you,' Jack suggested as he put down his table napkin and walked into the hall, where the telephone was installed on the wall above the umbrella stand. Esther only heard a muffled, one-sided conversation, then Jack returned, looking concerned.

'I spoke to Aunt Beattie, and she's beside herself,' he said. 'Apparently Percy's been missing for two nights.'

*

Percy looked up with an expression of burning resentment as the cell door opened, and in walked a stern-faced man in his late forties sporting a full beard and moustache that was as much grey in colour as the remaining vestiges of dark brown. He smiled coldly before speaking.

'So, the fabled Percy Enright broke the rules once too often, it seems, and this time he was not protected by the fact that he was a serving police officer. How did it feel to be cast into a cell like a common criminal?'

'Not all *that* common, to judge by the fact that I was allocated a cell to myself, and one that was actually above ground, allowing me to note the exchange of day for night. I calculate that I've been here for two days, during which time the food has been edible, but hardly enjoyable. If you knew who I was, why have I been held in here for that length of time, and not trundled in front of a magistrate?'

'Because you're not being charged with anything — this time, at least,' the man replied. 'Allow me to redress the balance in introductions. I'm Inspector Buxton, and you burgled the former residence of a murder victim whose death I'm currently investigating. If you stick your nose in my business one more time, you'll get what you deserve.'

'You know in your heart of hearts that Lucy Masefield's innocent,' Percy growled.

Buxton smiled coldly. 'I also know that she's your niece, which is why you're sniffing around trying to get her off, despite the evidence against her.'

'Do you seriously think that she'd use one of her own hatpins in order to construct a murder weapon, and then admit to it being her hatpin?'

'She doesn't have either your subtle brain or your familiarity with police procedures,' Buxton reminded him, 'and she just dropped herself in trouble without thinking.'

'And what motive did she have?' Percy challenged him. 'Her threat to cause Primrose to regret having challenged her abilities as a director was open to interpretation. All that she meant was that he wouldn't be getting any more parts in the plays she was putting on.'

'I'm not prepared to waste any more time arguing with you about this case,' Buxton insisted. 'Leave well enough alone, Percy, or you'll find yourself locked up for a lot longer than two days. And just so that you realise how cynically your niece played on your affections, you should know that I'll be charging her with the murder of Valentine Primrose by the end of the week. It's Monday morning, in case you'd lost track of the actual days. "Go thou and sin no more," as the Good Book says.'

With that he was gone. Less than thirty minutes later, Percy was escorted from his cell to the Charge Bar in the front hall of Bow Street Police Station and reunited with his possessions before being allowed back into the busy mid-morning street. When he returned home, he was met in the hallway by a stern-faced Beattie.

'Where have you been for the past three days, and why do you look as if you've been dragged through a hedge backwards?'

'It would take too long to explain, and either you wouldn't believe me, or you would, and then you'd treat me to one of your sermons. As it is, I need a bath, a change of clothes and one of your life-threatening breakfasts. The one starring eggs like cannonballs, bacon cooked to extinction, and toast with a film of carbon on both sides.'

It was rare for Percy to take that tone with her. Beattie looked as if she might shout in response, but instead simply replied, 'Esther needs to talk with you urgently.' She then slipped into the kitchen to prepare the demanded breakfast.

Two hours later, Percy was back in action and intent on gaining, by a lengthier and more lawful process, the same information that he'd tried to obtain by stealth. His first stop was at the Land Registry in Lincoln's Inn Fields. Not all titles to landed property were recorded here, but the more valuable ones were, and it was likely that large swathes of Mayfair and the West End had been recorded in this archive.

He filled in the form at the desk, then waited politely in the seat indicated until a clerk came out of a rear office and handed something to the desk attendant, who called Percy back and handed him the folder he'd requested. He glanced down for long enough to absorb the summary of its contents, then converted the oath that came to mind into a soft whistle.

Apartment Two, Addlebrook Mansions, Green Street, Mayfair was owned by none other than Regency Properties — the same Regency Properties that had solemnly told him, twice, that their 'client' was not interested in selling. The truth was that it was Regency Properties who were not interested in selling; he now needed to know who owned the company.

It was a short walk down Chancery Lane to the Companies Registry Office, where he failed to locate Regency Properties registered as a limited company. Then he followed his instinct and commissioned a search through the limited partnership records, and there it was. He let out an oath.

The registered partners of Regency Properties were none other than William Melville and Vernon George Waldegrave Kell — the two men who between them currently sat at the head of the nation's security services, and had no obvious legitimate reason for running a property enterprise. Clearly, Percy thought, the apartment in Green Street was maintained by them in just the same way, and for precisely the same reason, as the house in Tufnell Park Road. This then raised an interesting question regarding why the late Valentine Primrose had been residing in it. It might be a good idea to make a further check on other properties registered in the name of Regency Properties.

Ten minutes later he'd confirmed his suspicion regarding the house in Holloway, and had then opened his eyes wide in astonishment. There was what looked like half of Old Compton Street registered to the same organisation run by Britain's leading spymasters. He'd bet Belgravia to a brick that he'd already visited one of the properties in the block listed only as 'Nos. 137–145'. He now clearly needed to take himself down to Soho.

It was starting to rain as he stood across the road with a broad grin and read the numbers on the doors of an antique bookshop on one side, and a gentleman's outfitters on the other. One was numbered 137 and the other 141, so the blue door in the middle that gave access to 'Poppy's' must be 139. His national security puppet masters appeared to be the proprietors of a molly house, and he could hazard a confident guess as to why.

His next omnibus trip, this time one powered by a noisy, smelly internal combustion engine, took him to Spring Gardens, just off Trafalgar Square, where the London County Council, he knew from previous cases, maintained a registry of named proprietors of businesses within its jurisdiction. His final surprise of the morning came when he learned that Poppy's was the business concern of one Valentine Algernon Primrose. Or had been, until recently. Percy could only speculate whether or not the late Mr Primrose ever mixed with his clientele, and if so whether he'd ever had dealings with one of them named Mark Adlington.

Certain gentlemen in a certain house in Holloway owed him explanations, and he lost no time in taking yet another omnibus, this one drawn by a seemingly flatulent horse, to Mare Street, Hackney. There he ordered a pint and a meat pie in his favourite hostelry before making his way to his office, where a startled Rufus Tomkins looked up from his newspaper as his employer all but removed the front door from its frame in his anxiety to enter, cross the room, throw himself into his office chair and grab the telephone.

'I wish to consult with Mr Morgan urgently,' he announced to the faceless presence on the other end of the line, 'and if he can't fit me in immediately, I'll go somewhere else.'

He had an hour to wait before the coach would arrive. He first of all telephoned Jack to reveal what he'd learned, and obtain the telephone number of Cassiobury House School. He then made a call to Esther, who was summoned to the telephone by a very groggy-sounding Emily Allsop.

'Uncle Percy,' Esther asked 'where have you been for the past few days?'

'You wouldn't want to know,' Percy replied gruffly, 'but what did you have to tell me that was so urgent?'

'That WSPU that Simon Abelman's involved with, and that you talked me into joining — they're planning a protest march on Parliament on Wednesday, and I really don't want to get myself arrested. Not while I have all this extra responsibility at the school. I need to know whether I really have to attend or not.'

'Probably not,' Percy told, 'but think of a good excuse for missing it, like a sick child or something. I'll let certain people know what's being planned, so that they can respond accordingly. I'll be seeing them early this afternoon anyway. And how *is* Emily Allsop these days?'

'Getting weaker by the day. I think I may be the acting headmistress here for some time to come, I'm afraid.'

'Well, good luck with that, anyway. Jack will have some interesting news for you when he gets home. Now, I need to see a man about a molly house, so I'll speak to you later. Or is Sunday lunch out of the question these days?'

'Leave it with me, Uncle Percy. And try not to disappear like that again.'

'Before you get angry with me for having you kept in a cell for two days,' Melville began as Percy appeared, red-faced, in his office doorway, 'remember that it was also myself who ordered your release and instructed that there was to be no charge. You only have yourself to blame, Percy. What did you think you were playing at?'

'Obtaining information regarding why the apartment in Addlebrook Mansions was not being placed on the market,' Percy snapped. 'But then I made a few, more legitimate, enquiries, and now I know. Since when did property ownership come within your remit? Primrose was one of yours, wasn't he?'

'One of our what?' Melville asked, looking amused.

Percy finally let out the anger that had been welling up inside him ever since his release from a police cell. 'As usual you've been making my life difficult with half-truths in order to conduct your grubby trade! I'm leaving now — you can sort out this latest mess yourselves!'

'You're in danger of forgetting your niece,' Melville replied blandly, then consulted the fob watch that he extracted from his waistcoat pocket. 'It's almost time for afternoon tea and scones, so please join myself and Kell next door in the tea room.'

Ten minutes later, Percy had calmed down a little. 'Don't try and pressurise me by threatening to have Lucy charged with murder,' he warned Melville and Kell as he started angrily on his second scone, 'because Inspector Buxton already tried that and failed. You clearly don't believe that she did it, or else I wouldn't have been hired to find out who did, and Buxton himself has his doubts, I could tell. You just got him to pretend that Lucy's arrest is imminent in order to keep my nose to the grindstone, clearly. But I'd have got much further down the dirty path you pushed me into if you'd been honest in the first place. Primrose was one of yours, and you're out for revenge because someone stuck a knife in him.'

Melville looked meaningfully at Kell, who nodded, then turned back to Percy.

'Your task was, and still is, to find out who killed Primrose. Strictly speaking, the reason for this is none of your business. But since you've got this far, we concede that Primrose was indeed working for us, although not voluntarily. He was a wealthy homosexual with a long list of friends similarly inclined, and was caught frequenting an establishment staffed almost exclusively by men with the same preference. When we realised the extent of his network of contacts we offered him immunity from prosecution, with all the attendant embarrassing exposure, in return for his co-operation. We were by then aware that some of those working in sensitive areas of the Government might prefer the company of men, and were therefore vulnerable to blackmail. Primrose was placed by us in a certain establishment in Soho in which such persons might be quickly identified.'

'You mean Poppy's, of course,' Percy said with a glower. 'I'd worked that out for myself.'

'Then you might equally work out for yourself how the unfortunate demise of Primrose threw a spanner in our works,' Melville went on. 'The identification of his killer will not only secure some sort of compensation for the loss of his invaluable and unique services, but it will also highlight which of the sensitive areas of Government activity was most at risk. We already knew about Graves and Adlington, although thanks to your efforts we also learned that the latter was posing as "Joe Banks" in order, we believe, to assist Graves in doing away with Primrose. Quite how Graves got to realise that Primrose was working for us is a question to which we currently have no answer, but we still need you to ferret out the evidence that will lead Graves over the trapdoor.'

'So you no longer suspect Abelman?'

'Do you?' Melville asked.

Percy shrugged. 'I'm with you in the belief that the most likely suspect is Graves, but I wouldn't totally discount Abelman. Which reminds me: I've got Esther Enright on the inside of that WSPU mob, and she tells me that they're going to stage some sort of protest outside the Commons chamber on Wednesday of this week.'

'We'll deal with that in our own way,' Melville muttered as he took out a notebook and jotted something down in it, 'but let's stay focused on who killed Primrose. What do you propose to do next in order to have Graves buckled for it?'

'I already told you that it's up to you to sort out this mess,' Percy insisted fiercely.

'So you'll let your niece go to the gallows, just because you're too proud to admit that the task's proved too much for you?' Melville challenged him.

'That's not my reason, and you know it!' Percy shouted. 'It's because you've deceived me so much that I don't know what to believe, and I've done all I can with the limited assistance that you've given me. If you choose to take the task on yourselves from here, or if you can find some other dupe to drag into your spider's web of falsehood and double dealing, then you should know that the key to it all is probably the man calling himself "Joe Banks". The man you wouldn't have known was really Mark Adlington without my assistance.'

Kell and Melville exchanged glances, and it was Kell who spoke for them both.

'If we were to offer to suspend all further investigation into your niece's alleged involvement in Primrose's death, and instruct Buxton not to charge her with anything until you reveal the real killer, would that change your mind?'

'How do I know I can trust you?' Percy asked suspiciously.

'You don't, obviously,' Melville replied, 'but do you have any choice? And since when did Percy Enright admit defeat in a case?'

Percy stared at each of them in turn, then sighed. 'You're a tricky pair, but you have a point. But no more deception or withheld information, or you can find some other victim.'

CHAPTER FIFTEEN

'Very well, ladies, let's show them how loudly we can shout!' Constance Haywood yelled at the one hundred and fifty or so determined-looking women, each carrying a placard high in the air as they began their march, beginning with a one-hundred-yard stride to the junction of Caxton Street with Broadway. A right turn took them down it towards their intended target with clamorous calls of, 'Votes for Women!' and 'We've been kept silent for too long!' They swung left into Victoria Street, and less than a quarter of a mile later they came within sight of Parliament Square, where they came to a ragged halt in confusion.

The square had been painted dark blue with police uniforms, and everywhere they looked seemed to have been invaded by hulking bobbies in heavy greatcoats, armed with billy clubs. Constance turned to face her now wavering and anxious-looking troops and called out, 'Ignore those bullies! They can't stop us exercising our constitutional rights, remember! We have a right to communicate with our elected members, and if they won't listen to us inside the House, then they can be obliged to listen to what we have to say from the *outside*. Onward and upward, ladies!'

As Constance led the way, her banner held high, at least fifty women joined ranks and strode purposefully behind her. From the rear of the mass of uniformed bobbies rode a dozen mounted police on massive horses, whose riders nudged them into line at the head of their colleagues on foot, who raised their billy clubs to waist height in a threatening gesture.

Constance was the first to fall, forced onto the muddy ground by a sideways swipe from the rear end of a police horse. Before she could rise to her feet, she was grabbed by two uniformed bobbies and thrown into a police wagon that was parked to the side of the narrow opening into the square. Several of her friends and fellow campaigners uttered outraged protests and began assaulting the police line with their placards, most of which snapped in two when they came into contact with sturdy police helmets that were designed to withstand blows from far heavier weapons.

It was over in a matter of minutes, and thirteen members of the WSPU were hauled off to Cannon Row Police Station, where they had an appointment the following morning with the Bow Street Magistrate. Among them was Florence Bannister, who was visited by Simon Abelman the following morning in the noisy mass holding cell into which she'd been roughly bundled an hour earlier, despite the bandage around her head that was already leaking blood.

'What in God's name did they do to you?' Simon asked, horrified, as he looked at the bandage.

'I cut my head when a police horse pushed me to the ground,' Florence explained, 'but I was one of the lucky ones. Constance was knocked out cold, and Millie Watson thinks she may have broken her arm. Can you lodge claims on our behalf?'

Simon's face fell. 'I doubt it, to be perfectly honest, and I'm not even sure that I can get the charges dropped. Breach of the peace is one thing, but most of them have been charged with assaulting police officers, and the beak's likely to take a dim view of that.'

'*They* were the ones who assaulted *us*!' Florence replied angrily.

'It's going to be their word against yours, I'm afraid, and guess who the magistrate's more likely to believe? At least I can make bail applications for you all, and you're only charged with the breach, so you'll probably be getting off, with a bit of luck. But how did it all go so wrong?'

Florence frowned. 'Blame Constance. She assured us that there would only be a "token presence" of police outside Parliament House, but when we got there we were confronted by half the Metropolitan Police. The tallest and brawniest half, by the look of them, and they had no regard for the fact that they were handling women. In fact, Constance told me earlier that two of them were molested while they were in the back of the police wagons that they'd also got conveniently parked to one side of the square.'

'I can definitely make representations on their behalf about that,' Simon assured her, 'but what alarms me is the fact that the authorities clearly knew about your planned protest in advance. Someone must have alerted them to what you were intending.'

'Well, it wasn't me,' Florence asserted fiercely. 'If it had been, I wouldn't even have been there, and I wouldn't now have a cut on my head.'

Simon thought for a moment, then looked round the room in which most of the women were confined, some of them bearing physical evidence of having been in a skirmish with police officers. 'Where's Esther?' he asked.

'No idea. I don't even remember seeing her on the march — why?'

'Because someone betrayed us to the authorities, and it wouldn't surprise me to learn that it was her. She seemed altogether too willing to join the cause, yet when it came to the test, she doesn't seem to have put in an appearance. Perhaps she knew what was coming because she'd tipped off the police.'

'Well, you were the one who introduced her,' Florence reminded him, 'so if it turns out that she peached on us, then it's down to you.'

'I'm not saying that she did,' Simon replied, 'but I'll make it my business to find out.'

He had the opportunity to do so the following evening, Thursday, when the cast met for the line rehearsal of Act Three, which contained the famous "To be or not to be" speech by Hamlet, and his feigned madness as he rejects Ophelia. Esther was there, loyally reading the lines for Ophelia, and was a little intimidated by Lucy's long stares and apparent deep thought as she watched her performance. When the rehearsal was over, and given that Jack wasn't there, she was even more intimidated by Simon Abelman's demand to know why she'd missed the protest march the day before.

'One of my children was very sick,' she replied, having prepared the excuse in advance. 'The doctor was in and out all day, and poor little Miriam had a terrible fever, which mercifully seems to have subsided somewhat. My husband had some important business engagements, and I was the only one who could remain at home to look after our daughter. I understand from what I read in this morning's newspaper that there were some arrests.'

'Indeed there were, not to mention some substantial injuries, when the brutish police waded in with their billy clubs. You were fortunate to have missed it — or was that deliberate?'

'Of *course* it was deliberate!' Esther insisted with mock irritation. 'Didn't I just tell you that my daughter was ill?'

'Yes, you did,' Simon replied, 'but I'm not sure I believe that.'

'What other reason could I have had?'

'That's for you to know, and for me to find out,' Simon replied dismissively. 'And why couldn't you have left the child in the care of the nanny you told me about?' He paused, but before Esther could answer, he went on, 'But we'll leave it at that for now, shall we?'

Alice had been missing from the Thursday evening rehearsal, but when Esther turned up slightly early for the Saturday stage rehearsal of Act Three, she found that Alice had already arrived and was humming happily to herself as she laid out sandwiches in the kitchen.

'You seem very chipper today,' Esther remarked as Alice breezed back into the dressing room.

'Joe's invited me to meet his mother, and even to do some work for her,' she replied, grinning.

Alarmed, Esther reminded her, 'We *did* warn you about him, and particularly his — well, his lack of interest in women.'

'Perhaps I can change his mind,' Alice replied, her smile undiminished, 'and even if not, I'll be earning a little bit more helping her put her new place in order. She's moving from her current rooms in Bethnal Green to another, better, set, and she needs some cleaning done. Joe's taking me down there tomorrow, and who knows? Perhaps if his old mum approves of me, he'll start seeing me in a different light.'

'I very much doubt it, from what I know of people like that,' Esther warned her. 'And remember what else Jack and I told you about him. He's using an assumed name, which is never a good sign.'

'What do *you* know about life for someone like me?' Alice demanded, her smile gone. 'It's all right for you — you've got a loving husband and a family and all that. For lonely girls like me it's different, so don't even *think* of talking me out of it.'

Esther was desperately wishing that Jack could be here to hear what Alice was planning, and perhaps be more persuasive in convincing her to avoid Joe. But he wasn't in Act Three, and had chosen to go with Bertie to the latest display by the Hertfordshire Regiment on their parade ground up the road, in case it was a cover for a recruitment campaign. So Esther could only cross her fingers and hope that Alice didn't come to any harm, or perhaps betray what she knew of Esther and Jack's real identities.

The room soon began to fill with actors intent on proving that they'd learned all their lines for Act Three, and when they all moved onstage Esther was distracted by having to stand in for Ophelia, while Lucy called out Queen Gertrude's lines from the front row of the stalls.

'At least we're assured that Inspector Buxton won't be putting his hand on your shoulder for as long as Jack and I are on the case,' Percy assured Lucy on Sunday afternoon in Watford, as they gathered around the low table with cups of tea. Beattie was with the children in the garden, and it was time to bring everyone up to date.

'But from what you've just told us,' Esther commented, 'it seems that not even Melville and that other man were honest with you, even at the start. The man who died was one of their snoopers, and they're just out for revenge — isn't that the case? If so, are you carrying on with this just to preserve Lucy from being charged with something she didn't do?'

'Yes and no,' said Percy. 'Yes, in the sense that while I remain on the case there'll be no prospect of Lucy even being charged, let alone having to stand trial. And even were she to be proved not guilty after a trial, the taint would continue to hang over her name, so we need to prevent that. But there's also that side of me that won't let me admit defeat. So I have two reasons for battling on, although we seem to have come to something of a dead end. We strongly suspect either Graves or Abelman to have been the one behind Primrose's death, and we can be fairly sure that they were assisted "on the ground", so to speak, by Mark Adlington, who's calling himself "Joe Banks". But unless we can link one or more of them to Lucy's hatpin, we can't really drive home the guilt to any of them.'

'I'm pretty sure that Simon Abelman suspects me, and I'm very fearful that Alice will betray our secret to Joe,' Esther admitted softly. 'She's obviously still besotted with him, despite what we told her about him.'

'Well, don't for one moment think that I won't be eternally grateful to all of you for what you've done so far, even if you don't succeed in identifying the real culprit,' said Lucy.

'I've quite enjoyed it, really,' Jack said with a smile. 'All the hard work's been done by Percy. I've just indulged myself.'

'Well, you'll have to take that self-indulgence to a new level when we get to Act Five,' Lucy told him, 'and you have to fight a duel with Hamlet. I've arranged fencing lessons for you and Simon, since we don't want any more tragic deaths on stage. The rapiers you'll be using need to be handled very carefully.'

'When do these lessons begin?' Jack asked eagerly.

'You won't be so keen when I tell you that they'll be on Monday and Wednesday evenings, beginning at six o'clock and lasting until eight. You'll need to come straight from work, I imagine, and will need to eat at some local cook shop. It will also mean that you'll be away from home for four evenings a week, and the whole of Saturday. But that's the theatre for you — the closer you get to the actual performance date, the more the pressure increases, and the rehearsals become more and more frequent.'

'Good luck,' Esther said, laughing.

'Jack won't be the only one working his backside off,' said Lucy, turning to face her. 'I received word recently that the actress who'd promised to play Ophelia has just been diagnosed with a bad dose of the measles, and has been confined to her own home for at least the next six weeks. I've booked the other actors for the second week in September, and already commissioned the printing of all the publicity brochures and posters, so we have to stick to the originally planned opening night of Tuesday the twelfth, running through until Saturday the sixteenth.'

'So what are you going to do?' Esther asked.

'It's more a case of what *you're* going to do, Esther,' Lucy replied warmly. 'Or should I say "Ophelia"?'

Esther stared back with disbelief, then voiced her protest. 'You can't be serious! I mean, I'm hopeless, and I've only just been reading the part to help you out. I'm no actress!'

'I hate to disabuse you, but you are,' Lucy insisted. 'I've known about the problem for long enough to consider my options, and one of them was to let you develop in the role that you've been effectively understudying. I've been watching intently, and you have just that quality of ethereal disconnection, matched with natural beauty, that the role calls for. You've also read virtually all of it, since Ophelia dies by the end of Act Four. It's just a question of learning the lines.'

'Is that all?' Esther demanded sarcastically. 'On top of running a school, supervising a family and, almost as an afterthought, helping Jack and Percy find out who murdered the last actor to appear on your stage in the company of sharp weapons? Forget it, Lucy — that's really pushing family loyalty over the boundary.'

'Without Ophelia, there's no play,' Lucy reminded her.

'Then there's no play — it's as simple as that,' Esther said firmly.

Percy gave a polite cough. 'If I might be permitted to poke my oar in at this point? Without a play in rehearsal, we have no legitimate excuse for mixing with those we suspect of murdering Primrose, and therefore of proving Lucy's innocence. We've come this far, and can't abandon the chase now.'

'You were the one who said it had come to a dead end, or words to that effect,' Esther reminded him.

He nodded. 'All the more reason to push that little bit harder, and find out who could have stolen that hatpin. Esther, you'll need to prod Alice a little harder in the hope of triggering some memory.'

'Even assuming that she's still on our side once Joe's finished sweet-talking her,' Esther said with a grimace.

'And you'll take over the part of Ophelia?' Lucy asked anxiously.

Esther thought for a moment, then nodded. 'I suppose so. But if the production's a flop, don't blame me.'

CHAPTER SIXTEEN

It was a tense week for both Jack and Esther. Their most serious concern was the absence of Alice from all three rehearsals. While she might have had a legitimate reason for not attending the line rehearsals on weekday evenings, it had been her habit to do so, if only in the hope of being asked to read one of the parts that would be going to external actors for the final performances, or in order to see Joe. But there could be no rational reason for her absence from the Saturday stage rehearsals, where she was required in order to make notes of the characters' final positions on stage and assist in other ways, quite apart from supplying sandwiches from the bakery where she was employed. When someone from her workplace asked Lucy why Alice had been missing for the entire week, alarm bells began ringing, and Jack undertook to investigate whether Joe had had any part in Alice's disappearance.

There was also the increased pressure on Esther to master her lines, and she was feeling the strain of running a school virtually single-handed. Fortunately, the only other teacher, Doris Walker, had proved to be most efficient in the role of supervising Primary One and Two, leaving Esther free to manage the Senior Class while answering enquiries from the parents of potential new pupils.

The Saturday rehearsal was soon upon them, but fortunately Act Five didn't involve Ophelia, so Esther could take a back seat and watch carefully for any guilty behaviour on the part of those they were investigating. Her presence at the lunchbreak, and the continued absence of both Alice and the sandwiches she would have brought with her, gave Esther the excuse she needed to tackle Joe.

'I wish Alice had managed to get to today's rehearsals,' she commented casually. 'While these pork pies that Jack managed to get from that local bakery were adequate for our needs, they were hardly a substitute for Alice's delicious sandwiches. Do you happen to know where she's got to, Joe?'

'What makes you think that I'd know?' Joe replied guardedly.

'It's just that she mentioned to me that she was accompanying you on a visit to your mother last Sunday, and we haven't seen her since. Did she go with you as planned, and have you seen her this week?'

'No,' was his terse response.

'So how did it go?' Esther pressed him. 'Your mother was moving house, or so Alice said, and she had been hired to do some work for her.'

'That went as planned,' Joe replied, 'but the last I saw of her was when she left at about four o'clock to go home.'

'Where's the new house?' Jack asked as he sidled up to them to join the conversation. 'Still in Bethnal Green?'

'Yes — Gosset Street.'

'I know that area,' Jack replied. 'Isn't most of it condemned to make room for new housing being erected by the LCC?'

'Yes,' Joe said, visibly unsettled. 'That's why she was moving — she's got one of the new houses.'

'I wasn't aware that they'd started construction,' Jack probed. 'She must be one of the lucky ones. Or maybe you have a friend on the LCC. Are you keeping a dark secret from us?'

'What are you getting at?' Joe suddenly flared up. 'What am I being accused of?'

'It was just a joke, sorry,' said Jack, and this time the response came from Ernest Graves, who needn't have been at the rehearsal in the first place, since his character, Polonius, had been killed off by Act Five.

'Leave the boy alone, for God's sake. Can't you see that you're making him uncomfortable?'

'I didn't mean anything by it,' Jack insisted, feigning innocence and embarrassment.

'Yes, you bloody did!' Joe exploded, despite a warning glare from Ernest. 'You were hinting that I might have done away with Alice. Next thing you'll be accusing me of stealing hatpins — just keep your bloody thoughts to yourself, and concentrate on being Laertes. You certainly need all the practice you can get!'

With that he stormed out of the dressing room, leaving Ernest with a horrified expression on his face, and Jack exchanging meaningful looks with Esther.

'Sorry about that, everyone,' he muttered. 'Joe's right — I should keep a tighter rein on my mouth.'

The following day, Sunday, the family gathered in the Watford house.

'He really dropped a brick once I goaded him a little,' Jack reported gleefully over pre-lunch drinks while Beattie supervised the children's hand-washing. 'Why else would he make specific reference to hatpins? And what got him really rattled was Esther's probing into what might have become of Alice.'

'It was fortunate that you knew all about those demolitions in Bethnal Green,' Esther added.

Jack chuckled. 'I didn't, as it happens — that was pure bluff. I knew that there had been some further north, but I've no idea whether they're demolishing Gosset Street or not. And clearly, Joe didn't either, so what's happened to Alice?'

'It's my job to find out,' Percy volunteered. 'But I have an uneasy feeling that the outcome of my enquiries won't be a happy one.'

'Anything would help, at this stage,' Jack told him. 'But at least we can now work on the assumption that it was Joe who stole the hatpin. But who for?'

'Ernest Graves was very quick to try and rescue Joe when he began foaming at the mouth,' Esther reminded him. 'Perhaps it was Graves who put him up to it.'

'He's always been one of our leading suspects,' Percy agreed, 'but how did Abelman react?'

'He didn't, so far as I can recall,' Esther replied, 'but then he'd exhausted himself during the rehearsal, pretending to duel with Jack.'

'That reminds me, Jack — your fencing lessons begin tomorrow evening,' Lucy put in. 'Six o'clock sharp. And I'm paying for your lessons by the hour, so don't be late.'

Just then the sitting room door opened, and Beattie entered the room with a wry smile.

'This Shakespeare nonsense seems to have affected the entire family. The children were taking it in turns to wash their hands when dear little Annabelle suddenly started wringing her hands and rambling on about spots of blood. When I asked her what she was drivelling on about, she said it was from Shakespeare.'

Lucy laughed. 'That was from *Macbeth*. Lady Macbeth has a sleepwalking scene in which she's washing imaginary blood from her hands after the murder of King Duncan. Clearly I have another budding actress I can call on in the future.'

'Don't you dare!' Beattie protested. 'This acting nonsense has caused enough trouble for this family already. Percy, it's roast lamb for lunch, so mind and leave some for the others.'

*

Percy walked into Bethnal Green Police Station the following morning, hoping that no-one would remember a former sergeant who'd broken all the rules during his brief stint there.

'Can I help you, sir?' asked the fresh-faced constable behind the desk.

'I hope so, young man,' Percy replied amiably. 'My name is Percival, and I'm a private enquiry agent. I'm acting — free of charge, I might add, out of a sense of public duty — for the relatives of a young lady who's gone missing in this area. She disappeared over a week ago, after she went to answer an advertisement for a sales assistant's position in a clothing shop in Bethnal Green Road. It's feared that she may have met with a grisly end, and the family have asked me to enquire whether or not any bodies of young women have been discovered on your patch.'

'I'll need to refer your enquiry to Inspector McLean,' the constable replied. 'Just take a seat over there, and I'll have him brought down to speak with you.'

Ten minutes later Percy looked up with a smile as he heard a familiar voice.

'Percy Enright, you tricky old bugger! What are you up to this time? Come to steal the biscuits from the tea room?'

'So Jock McLean made it to Inspector despite being partnered with me for the best part of a year,' Percy said warmly as he recalled their days as constables in Hackney. 'So who did you bribe?'

'You'd know all about greasing the wheels, Percy,' said Jock with a grin. 'The number of times you got away with ignoring the Procedures Manual! So what brings you down here? You've surely been thrown out of the Met by now, since they've long since tightened up the disciplinary processes.'

'I retired with full colours,' Percy told him, 'and at the same rank as you. I'm now a private enquiry agent, and I'm looking for a young woman's body, unfortunately. She's called Alice Bennett, and is believed to have been lured down here over a week ago. The name "Gosset Street" was mentioned, but she could have ended up in the Thames, on the back of a goods train, or under a coal tip in the docks. Anything you can give me will be a help.'

'We did get one a while ago,' Jock recalled. 'Someone reported hearing a woman screaming inside a deserted tenement, and from memory it *was* in Gosset Street. We sent a couple of constables to investigate, and they found the corpse of a woman in her mid-twenties, strangled to death, and clearly molested. No-one's claimed her body yet, so she may be the one you're after. Do you have a photograph?'

'Only head and shoulders, and a bit blurry, but probably good enough for your purposes. Did you actually see the body?'

'No, but she's still in our makeshift mortuary down the road. I can give you a chitty to view it, and when you get back it'll be time for you to buy me a pint at the Crown in exchange for a gander at our file.'

Thirty minutes later, Percy needed only one look at the woman's body to know she was Alice. He turned away sadly as he wondered how he would break the bad news to Jack, Esther and Lucy. Then he kept his promise to meet Jock at the Crown.

Once they had their drinks, Jock opened the file. 'The bloke who heard the screams and reported them also saw someone walking quickly up the street, away from their source. His name's Tom Parkinson, and here's his address. He's a respectable type who works as a coal heaver in the docks. He can probably tell you more.'

The sun was beginning to set by the time Percy was waiting for Tom Parkinson as he strolled purposefully into the common court that gave access to his tenement dwelling three streets away from the police station. He was covered in coal grime, and nodded when Percy asked him to confirm his identity, then held out a five pound note. Since this was over twice the man's weekly wage during the good times, he was more than content to stop for a moment while Percy showed him a series of head-and-shoulders photographs of Jack, Simon Abelman, Ernest Graves, Leopold Carter and Joe Banks. The man squinted, then pointed to the image of Joe Banks.

'That 'un. Definitely 'im. An' thanks fer the fiver.'

As Percy made his way back to the station, he reflected on what he'd learned. He could now close in on Mark Adlington for the murder of Alice Bennett. And there was always the chance that Adlington would be prepared to dodge the noose in exchange for something of even greater value.

On Monday evening, Jack and Simon arrived at the theatre for their first fencing lesson. They stood on stage, while Lucy watched from the front row.

'First of all, your weapon,' said Pierre Ravisson, the French-born tutor who had been hired by Lucy. 'It is called a "foil", and it is designed to hit the opponent only with the tip, and not by any slashing motion, as it would be with a sword. You move backwards and forwards using mainly your feet, and your hand is merely used in order to grip the foil, thus.'

He demonstrated a forward lunge with his arm crooked at the elbow until the final moment, when he straightened it in order to deliver an imaginary blow. 'From this you will see that it is all done with the movement of the feet, and it is therefore with the feet that we must begin our first lesson. Regard.'

He stood with his feet at right angles to each other, the right foot pointing directly forward, and the left foot at ninety degrees to the right foot. 'I will assume that you are both right-handed,' he said as he took a sharp step forward with his right foot and thrust into empty space. 'If I have judged my distance correctly, I have just scored a hit on my opponent,' he announced, 'and then in order to retreat, I use my left foot as the means by which I pull back. Now each of you show me how you imitate these actions.'

They spent the next hour perfecting the thrust, parry and retreat actions until they were as proficient as could be expected for a pair of amateur actors.

Lucy stood up. 'Now we need to incorporate the necessary stage directions, and Pierre can advise on those as well,' she said. 'There's a very complex climax to the play, so listen carefully. Laertes has planned to kill Hamlet by dipping his foil point in poison. He manages to score a hit on Hamlet, then somehow the blades become exchanged. Pierre can tell us how that can be achieved in a moment. But Hamlet ends up with the poisoned blade and scores a hit on Laertes, so now they're both destined to die.'

Jack and Simon stood in the poses they had been taught, each of them wondering how to proceed.

'I suggest a few lunges and parries to begin with,' said Lucy. 'Then Laertes lunges forward and manages to land a blow on Hamlet. That's when he says, "Have at you now," Hamlet will need to stagger back a little, to make it clear to the audience that he's been wounded.'

Jack looked down apprehensively at the tip of his foil.

'The tips are covered by rubber caps, for your protection, so don't worry. I checked them before rehearsal,' Lucy reassured him.

'I hope you made a better job of it than you did with the knives for *Julius Caesar*,' Jack muttered.

Lucy frowned. 'That wasn't even remotely funny, Jack. Now get on with it.'

Jack did as instructed, and after a minute or two of mutual puffing and blowing he managed to land a blow on Simon's chest. Simon winced as he stepped backwards and complained, 'I felt that! Not a cut, obviously, but I bet I'll have a bruise there in the morning. Now what?'

'We need to stage the exchange of the foils, so that Laertes can get poisoned with the same blade — "hoist with his own petard", as Shakespeare said in Act Three, if you recall,' said Lucy. 'Now, Pierre, what's the best way to stage this?'

'Well,' Pierre replied thoughtfully, 'sometimes, when the adversaries both lunge at the same time, the foils become joined at the hilts — they're the round bits that protect your hands. In an effort to untangle them, the players thrust upwards, and if they lose their grips the foils can fly backwards into the air — this way.' He demonstrated. 'If the two actors could push forward as well as upwards, they will then stumble forward and pick up the foils that were previously in the hands of their opponents. In this way, they end up with each other's foils. You understand what I am describing?'

Jack and Simon nodded, and Lucy urged them to try what Pierre had just suggested. On their third attempt they succeeded, and Lucy clapped her hands in delight.

'Excellent! Let's do that a few more times, then call it a day, shall we? We'll come back on Wednesday and see how much you boys have remembered.'

On Wednesday it was soon apparent that Jack and Simon had taken their first lesson to heart, and after an hour or so Lucy declared herself satisfied with their progress. 'We'll do the whole of Act Five at Saturday's rehearsal, and incorporate the duel scene. Then if it needs any further rehearsal or practice, we'll meet again next Monday and Wednesday. I just hope that Alice is here to help Joe with the chalk markings, because the positions of the two duellists will be crucial to the staging of the dramatic finale.'

The following Sunday, Percy told Lucy what had happened to Alice.

'I saw her body — there's no doubt that it was her. I'm sorry, Lucy,' he said sadly.

Esther wiped a tear from her cheek. 'The poor girl only wanted someone to love her! I tried to warn her against Joe, but I couldn't give her the whole story of how we suspected him of being involved in the murder of Primrose. I even warned her that the story of Joe's elderly sick mother was just that — a story — but nothing would stop her from pursuing her dearest wish. And now she's dead, and I can't help blaming myself!'

'You can't afford to think like that,' Lucy told her sternly, wiping her own eyes. 'Everyone must eventually take responsibility for their own lives.'

'Are you really sure we should be pushing ahead with the play?' Jack asked. 'We're all still a bit rusty, as you know, and we don't want to give a bad performance when we finally open for the public.'

'Dress rehearsals have a habit of ironing out all the creases,' Lucy responded, 'and I know I can rely on you and Esther to give it your all. I've been rehearsing with the borrowed actors on Sundays, and I think you'll find that they'll blend in perfectly.'

'Do you mind if I attend the dress rehearsal on Saturday?' Percy asked. 'I'll do my "theatrical journalist" impersonation again.'

'Why would you want to do that?' Jack asked. 'It'll be very boring for you, surely?'

'I hope so,' Percy said solemnly, 'but just in case it isn't, I want to be there.'

CHAPTER SEVENTEEN

'Well, let's all give it our best shot,' Lucy urged the actors as they gathered in the dressing room ahead of the Saturday dress rehearsal. 'Remember, whatever goes wrong, we just keep going. And it's particularly important that we get it right, because Mr Pierrepoint has very generously agreed to watch the entire rehearsal, then give us much-needed publicity in the local papers ahead of the opening in two weeks' time. The ticket sales have been very disappointing so far, and we don't want to be playing to empty houses.'

'I'd rather be playing in the living room of my *own* house,' Jack muttered to Esther as he tried to lift his chin above the ornate ruff around his neck. 'These tights feel like they're going to cut off the blood supply to my legs, and as for this stupid thing under my chin, it's bound to choke me before the end of the second act.'

'I don't know what you're complaining about,' Esther said with a frown, 'since it'll be a miracle if I don't fall flat on my face in this fancy ballgown. It weighs half a ton with all those sequins I sewed onto it, little knowing that I'd be the one wearing the damned thing, and before the opening night I'll definitely have to raise the hem on it.'

'I think you look *very* elegant,' Jack said, smiling. 'A pity you're supposed to be my sister, because I quite admire you in all that finery. Ophelia never looked so beautiful, and Laertes never felt so clumsy.'

'I just hope I can remember my lines,' Esther said, sighing, 'else Uncle Percy will never let me hear the end of it. Why did he insist on being here, anyway?'

'He never said,' Jack replied. 'Whatever devious game he's playing, he's playing it close to his chest.'

'Very well, everyone,' Lucy called out. 'On stage for Act One, Scene One, as we rehearsed it, and the rest of you who are in Scene Two go into the wings, please. I'm in the first scene, so don't expect any more directing from me; this evening I'm just one of the cast.'

Jack was even more nervous this time than he had been when undergoing his audition as Laertes, but fortunately his only speech in the first scene went without a hitch. He was then able to retire into the wings and watch the rest of them, including the borrowed actors from the Chelsea company, perform their parts with remarkable skill, given their relatively short rehearsal time during the previous weeks.

As they moved smoothly into Act Two, it was Esther's turn to suppress her nerves as she gave a creditable performance as Ophelia, startled and a little frightened by Hamlet's strange behaviour. She rose to the challenge, and even to Jack's untutored eyes and ears she seemed to be carrying off her part with aplomb, and he began to relax.

There was a scheduled interval following the end of Act Three, and a predictable queue for the lavatories, then everyone gathered back in the dressing room for glasses of lemonade and a few sandwiches brought in by Lucy. Jack was just reflecting on how much better the sandwiches had been when poor Alice had been supplying them when he caught sight of Percy, in his assumed role as Francis Pierrepoint, talking animatedly to Simon Abelman. He waited until they parted company, then sidled up to Percy.

'I still don't know why you're here,' he muttered, 'except to see me make a fool of myself.'

'All may be revealed in the final act,' Percy muttered as he nodded to Ernest Graves and made to walk towards him across the crowded and noisy dressing room. Just before moving away from Jack he turned and said, 'Your fencing skills will need to be of the finest, if my hunch proves correct.'

'What hunch?' Jack demanded, but Percy had moved on.

'Very well, Act Four — places everyone!' Lucy called out, and they all made their way into the wings, where Joe was ready to winch open the curtain on a waved command from Lucy. This was the big dramatic moment for both Esther and Jack. Esther gave her performance as the mad Ophelia as if she'd been rehearsing for it all her life, while Jack stomped and raved as the enraged Laertes, and set the scene perfectly for the final act, and the duel scene in which even Shakespeare had outdone himself with the number of deaths onstage. As the curtain closed for the end of the act, then opened again almost immediately for the start of Act Five, Jack looked down into the empty front row, where Percy had spent the previous acts, half wondering where he'd got to. Then he concentrated on making his part in the final scene as dramatic as he could.

The fencing foils had been lying on a side table in the wings, and were brought onstage by two of the supporting actors in their roles as courtiers while Laertes and Hamlet stood glowering at each other. Jack had his back to the wings on the left of the stage, with Simon Abelman facing him from stage right, as they began their duel with the ritual waving of foils. Then it was into the feint, parry, thrust and retreat movements that they'd practised to perfection, up to the moment when the foil hilts became tangled, then flew apart. As planned, Jack's foil clattered across the stage behind him and slid across the boards towards the stage left wings, where Joe was waiting to retrieve it and slide it back to Simon, as planned. Then Simon turned and raced towards Jack with his foil pointed directly at his chest, as they moved towards the part of the scene where Laertes was to be dealt a mortal blow by Hamlet.

Jack was aware of a struggle taking place in the wings, but needed to concentrate hard on the remainder of the duel. Then he heard a yell from Percy: 'Avoid the sword!' Taking it to be a reference to the foil, Jack looked carefully at the weapon in Simon's hand, then froze in horror. The rubber tip that was meant to ensure his safety had somehow been dislodged, and he was now genuinely fighting for his life.

All pretence of sticking to the script was abandoned as Jack backed further and further towards the stage right wings, with Simon advancing on him with a determined glint in his eyes. With a final leap Jack managed to get behind the heavy drape, and threw its leading edge as hard as he could towards Simon's extended foil tip. It somehow managed to snare it, and as Simon cursed and tried to disentangle it he was felled by a flying leap from Percy, who had raced across the stage from the far left.

'What's going on here?' cried Lucy, who was supposed to be in the process of dying in her role as Queen Gertrude.

Once Percy had Simon pinned to the stage boards, Jack rushed to help him. From his jacket pocket Percy extracted a set of hand restraints, and a loudly cursing Simon was held down by Jack. Percy rose quickly and raced back across the stage, only to be met by a couple of rough-looking individuals who had Joe Banks in a firm grip, with both arms up his back.

'We caught him running out through the stage door, just as you predicted, sir,' one of them said. 'And he struggled a bit, which is why he can't see too well out of his left eye.'

'Take him to Hackney Police Station, have him charged with murder, and tell the desk sergeant that I'll be there to explain everything in the morning,' Percy instructed them. 'Then come back for this one, who's to be taken to Melville in the Tufnell Park house.'

'Very good, sir,' the man replied, as he lifted Joe Banks clean off his feet by the arms that were pinioned behind his back. His screams of pain grew fainter as he disappeared from sight.

Lucy had risen to her feet, and as she stood by Percy's side, looking down at where Jack was continuing to pinion Simon to the boards, she asked, 'Presumably you had a good reason for all that, Uncle Percy? You just ruined a perfectly running dress rehearsal.'

'This bastard tried to kill me!' Jack shouted back as he lifted his head. 'Take a closer look at that foil that's stuck in the curtain.'

Lucy did as instructed, then let out a horrified cry. 'The safety plug's fallen off it!'

'It was *pulled* off it,' Percy told her. 'I was watching from behind Joe in the wings, and Abelman threw the weapon far enough to reach Joe, who was waiting for it. He then pulled the safety device off the tip of the blade and sent it back onstage. It was clearly meant to look like another tragic accident.'

'I had a narrow escape,' Jack added as he kneed Simon in the ribs, 'thanks to my eagle-eyed uncle.'

'This man is your uncle?' Henry Gloucester asked as he ceased pretending to be King Claudius and rose from his chair on the stage. 'I thought he was a theatre journalist.'

'That's what you were meant to think,' Percy told him. 'And you weren't to know that young Jack here is a chief inspector at Scotland Yard, while the beautiful Ophelia is his wife, and Lucy is his sister. Only one other person associated with this theatre, apart from the four of us, knew our true identities. She was murdered two weeks ago, which is why she's been absent.'

'Alice?' Henry exclaimed, his hand to his mouth. 'Oh, how *awful!* How did *that* happen?'

'I'm saying no more until we get Abelman back on his feet and removed to the safety of certain premises a little distance from here, in which he will be suitably interviewed. I'll give you all the full story in due course, when I know it. In the meantime, Jack, keep our prisoner firmly nailed to the floor.'

It was almost an hour later before the two burly men returned and told Percy that Joe Banks was now available for interview in Hackney Police Station.

'Take Abelman to meet Mr Morgan,' Percy instructed, scribbling down an address. 'Tell Morgan to leave enough of him for me to interrogate some time tomorrow, and to have the coach pick me up outside my business premises at twelve noon.'

'So what do we do now?' Jack asked as he rose to his feet and dusted down his costume.

'I suggest that you and Esther get changed and make your way home. And call for me no later than nine tomorrow morning,' said Percy.

'It's too late for the train,' Esther pointed out, 'and we'd sort of assumed that we could stay overnight with Lucy.'

Lucy smiled. 'Of *course* you may. I arranged for a late supper for when I got home from the dress rehearsal. Although today may have been a waste of time, as matters transpired, unless I can find another willing actor who can learn Hamlet's part in less than two weeks.'

'I think you'll be missing at least one other leading actor by then,' Percy told her without looking at anyone in particular. 'So, much though it pains me to say it, *Hamlet* just got cancelled. All those rehearsals in vain, but at least you can console yourself with the thought that you're no longer a murder suspect. I'll travel with Jack at eight in the morning in a borrowed coach, and we can interview a certain Mr Adlington after he's benefitted from a night in the cells.'

The following morning, a coach rumbled to a halt outside Lucy and Teddy's premises in Southampton Row, where Jack stood waiting, and Percy poked his head through the window. 'In you get, Jack my boy,' he called jovially, 'and let's see how Mr Adlington is faring after a night in his own company, and a very frugal breakfast.'

As they strolled smugly through the front door of Hackney Police Station, the desk sergeant gave them an angry glare. 'This isn't a dumping ground, even if you *were* once the same rank as me in here. Inspector Tasker wants to see you, and your prisoner's calling for his lawyer every ten minutes.'

'We've got *him* in custody as well,' said Percy, 'but assuming that the Inspector's been served his morning tea, we'll just trot up there and join him.'

As soon as Percy and Jack appeared in his doorway, Tasker demanded, 'What's going on, Percy? If it had been anyone else issuing the orders, I'd have refused custody of the man calling himself "Banks". And who's he supposed to have murdered?'

'His real name is Mark Adlington, and he murdered a young woman called Alice Bennett in Bethnal Green a couple of weeks ago. Or at least, he arranged for it to happen. And we think he committed another murder months ago, so all I need is a nice uncomfortable room in which to apply the blowtorch, then you can book him through the local magistrates' court and have him sent down to Pentonville.'

'Use the one below ground level,' said Tasker, 'and just out of interest, who were those two apes who brought Banks in here?'

'They're employed by a Government department that's so secret that not even the Government knows about it,' Percy told him. 'Now, if you'd excuse us?'

Down in one of the grimmest interrogation rooms that Jack had ever encountered, Mark Adlington was seated at a badly scarred metal table, his wrists manacled and resting on the table in front of him. He looked up with a frown of resentment as Percy and Jack entered.

'Who exactly *are* you two, and why am I being held here?' Adlington demanded.

'You don't need to know who I am,' Percy replied with exaggerated sweetness, 'except that, as you've probably worked out for yourself, I'm not a theatre journalist. But with the photograph I managed to con you out of, I was able to confirm from a reliable witness that you were seen hastily leaving a set of premises in which the *much* abused body of Alice Bennett was later found. As for my companion here — the one you know only as "Jack Evans", an aspiring actor — he's a Chief Inspector at Scotland Yard, and the older brother of the woman you tried to implicate in the murder of Valentine Primrose.'

'That wasn't me!' Adlington protested. 'You can't do me for that one!'

'I may not do you for the *other* one, if you're prepared to engage in a deal to save your miserable neck,' Percy told him. 'Whether you call yourself "Joe Banks" or use your real name, it will be all the same to the public executioner. He's called Billington, and he normally does a very efficient job.'

'So what's the deal?' Adlington asked quickly.

'You talk, and we listen,' said Percy. 'It's very simple, but hopefully very enlightening. Start with who put you up to stealing the knife that was used to kill Valentine Primrose.'

An hour later, Percy called a halt outside a cook shop a few doors up Mare Street from the police station that they'd just left.

'I imagine that Lucy provided you both with an adequate early breakfast before Esther had to catch the train back to Watford, but my breakfast came courtesy of your Aunt Beattie, so guess what I'm ready for now?'

'A proper breakfast?' Jack suggested with a smile, and ten minutes later they were each polishing off a plate of bacon and eggs.

'Since we have a little while to talk before you have to catch that coach,' Jack said as he cleared his mouth, 'how did you manage to anticipate that Abelman would try to kill me?'

'Logic,' said Percy. 'I assumed that poor Alice had betrayed you to whoever was controlling Adlington, and he's just confirmed that that was indeed Abelman. I was suspicious about him, but I couldn't be sure. So it was simply a matter of guessing how whoever it was would set about taking you off the boards, so to speak. The obvious ploy was to stage another tragic accident, and when I learned that you were to fight a duel with one of our suspects, employing fencing foils with tips protected by detachable plugs, it became obvious. I asked Lucy how the scene was to be staged, then slipped behind Adlington at the crucial moment, and caught him in the act.'

'Thank goodness that you did!' Jack exclaimed. 'But how do you intend to justify the deal you offered?'

'He's more than happy to peach on Abelman and Graves in exchange for just being charged as an accessory to the murder of Primrose and the attempt on your life. With a recommendation for clemency, he should be out in a few years.'

'That wasn't quite what I meant,' Jack objected. 'He murdered Alice Bennett.'

'Did he?' Percy challenged him. 'The only witness we have against him can only testify that he saw Adlington walking away from the scene at the same time that he heard screams from a woman who *might* have been Alice. We can't prove definitely that it was her, and even if we could, clearly he wasn't there when she was actually being killed. The worst that he's guilty of, in the eyes of your average jury, is callous indifference. He's prepared to plead guilty to taking her to the house in the hope that his associates — common thugs, he said — could frighten the truth out of her. He'll say that he then panicked and abandoned her when they became more violent than he'd intended. Again, that will earn him a few years behind bars, hopefully served at the same time as he's serving the sentence for his activities in Lucy's theatre.'

'I wish you luck in persuading the men you've been working for to accept all that,' Jack replied gloomily.

'Well, you'll be there to observe it, Jack my boy, because you're going with me, to back me up.'

CHAPTER EIGHTEEN

'Who told you you could bring *him*?' Melville demanded testily as Percy and Jack were admitted into his office, in which Kell was already installed behind the same desk.

'*He* is my nephew Jack, who's played as important a role as anyone in uncovering the truth behind the murder of Valentine Primrose,' Percy replied tersely. 'Thanks to his bravery in allowing himself to be used as a target for that dangerous bunch posing as actors, we now have two of them ready for whatever you have planned for them.'

'I'm told that you have Adlington locked away in some obscure cell,' said Melville. 'Why wasn't he brought here along with Abelman?'

'I didn't want you to have all the fun,' said Percy, smiling. 'Are we too early for afternoon tea? If so, perhaps we could while away the time exchanging our findings. Adlington's ready to peach on Abelman and Graves, if anyone knows where he can be found.'

'I assume you did one of your dirty deals?' Melville said, frowning. 'The ones for which you were unjustifiably famous during your Met days? How much has it cost us in potential prosecutions?'

'Adlington will admit to being an accessory to the murder of Primrose, in exchange for not taking the drop for the murder of Alice Bennett.'

'We already have Abelman's elegant hand on the dotted line,' Melville said grimly, 'as the result of an interrogation that kept us up half the night. He dropped Graves into trouble as well, so it wasn't really necessary for you to offer a deal to

Adlington. Another good reason why he should have been delivered to us, and not left to contemplate the ambience of a sordid cell in Hackney. But I suppose you meant well.'

'So what did Abelman reveal about who did what?' Percy asked. 'Or is that to remain a closely guarded State secret?'

'I suppose you're entitled to know,' Melville conceded after a nod from Kell, 'since you did some of the minor legwork. It all begins with Primrose's excellent work for us as the notional proprietor of Poppy's.'

'He was sniffing out men who might pose a security risk, if I recall correctly?' Percy asked. 'And if this is likely to take much longer, might we be allowed to take a seat?'

'Let's move next door,' Kell suggested, 'and we'll organise an early afternoon tea, so you can attempt to exceed your previous nauseating record for the consumption of sponge cake. Bring your nephew with you, since we wouldn't want to leave him in here unsupervised.'

Seated around a low table equipped with tea, biscuits and cake, Melville picked up where Percy had left off.

'Primrose, as you already know, was running Poppy's for us. He introduced his partner Leopold Carter as a member, since Carter was more adept at, shall we say, "attracting" just the sort we were anxious to catch. By this means he brought us information about Graves, a man who made no secret of either his sexual preferences or his sensitive work at the Admiralty. We were preparing to bring the hammer down on him when he — Graves, that is — introduced his "close friend" and work colleague Mark Adlington, and suddenly we knew how Graves had gained access to the *Dreadnought* plans. Then Abelman walked into the picture, and we chose to delay hauling in Graves and Adlington in the hope that we could learn more about the growing unrest regarding women's demands for voting rights — which, added to the mounting rumbles regarding Irish Home Rule, was causing our Government some inconvenience and discomfort.'

'But Abelman isn't interested in men, surely?' Jack chipped in. 'He has a lady friend who's probably his lover — a woman called Florence Bannister.'

'We obviously knew all about the woman, and you're right about Abelman. However, he's a leading figure in a very covert network of influential and able lawyers who're committed to causing as much domestic upheaval as possible within the nation, we believe at the behest of the German Kaiser. He successfully defended Adlington when he was caught in a molly house, and Adlington told Carter about him, in case Carter required the same sort of service in the future. As it transpired he didn't, because — as you discovered by means of entirely illegal actions — Carter was the regular live-in partner of Primrose.

'Somehow or other — and this remains a mystery to us, although you might wish to investigate further — Abelman learned that Primrose was reporting back to us and flushing out those who might be a security risk because of their homosexual preferences, which would leave them open to blackmail. He was apprehensive that this might involve the WSPU, of whose existence Adlington was aware, and had revealed to Carter. So, after taking instruction from those at the centre of his little "civil disruption" club, Abelman set about silencing our man Primrose.'

'Employing Graves?' Percy asked, and Melville nodded.

'Graves *and* Adlington, as it turned out. Abelman was a keen amateur actor, and when he learned that Primrose was a member of the Holborn Players, of which your niece Lucy is a leading light, he joined for himself, then encouraged Graves to do so when Lucy chose *Julius Caesar* for her next production, and he realised that there was an assassination scene.'

'So it was Abelman who came up with the idea of doctoring a knife, and he got Adlington to steal one from the props cupboard?' Percy asked.

'That much was perhaps obvious, even to you,' Melville replied unkindly. 'What we didn't know was how Carter was duped into taking it onstage, where it was used to deadly effect. Using Primrose's own partner to actually deliver the blow was especially diabolical. We were hoping that you could work out how the last-minute switching of knives was achieved, but as it happens Abelman was most obliging on that score.'

'We're finally at the bit that most interests me,' said Percy, 'so please enlighten me.'

'Adlington was instructed to steal one of Lucy Masefield's hatpins, which Abelman himself pushed up through the release mechanism in order to jam it. He did that earlier on the day of the final performance, then made sure that it was Adlington who laid out the "safe" knives on the table, thereby ensuring that Mrs Masefield wasn't aware that there were only two left in the props cupboard, and was able to check the five for safety. This left Abelman with the doctored knife, and since he'd noticed that Carter always had stomach trouble before going on stage, he was the obvious one to plant the fatal knife on.'

'I'm a little confused,' Percy muttered. 'How did Abelman manage the switch?'

'Bluff and bluster, as befits a windbag like him,' Melville said dismissively. 'He made a big dramatic gesture of leading the rest of the "conspirators" on stage, then slipped back under the pretence of having left his own knife behind, hoping that Carter would still be on the toilet, which of course he was.

Then when Carter returned, Abelman harassed him into taking the doctored knife, which he made sure was the only one left after he pretended to pick up the other one, although of course he still had the one that he'd originally taken on stage. He hurried Carter onstage ahead of him, and dropped the spare one onto the table. Then once they were all back on stage, the spare was left for Alice to find and put back into the props cupboard, making up the remaining three that Lucy found in there when she checked under the eagle eye of Inspector Buxton. By the way, he's been told that the murderer has been identified and will be dealt with, so Lucy Masefield is no longer a suspect. You achieved what you set out to do, Percy.'

'I achieved what *you* wanted me to do,' Percy said, frowning, 'but it all worked out well in the end. What do you intend to do with Graves, assuming that you ever find him?'

'He turned up for work today, bold as brass,' said Kell, 'and was immediately apprehended and taken into custody by the military authorities. On my instruction, they were prepared to let him off with mere dismissal, and no capital charge of spying for Germany, provided that he revealed who his contact was. This will no doubt come as a surprise to you, Percy: it was Arthur Dennistoun, who used his regular trips to Vienna in connection with his art dealing business as a cover for slipping valuable documents to a German contact he had there. When he'd been charged with art fraud some years ago, he'd been successfully defended by Abelman, and it was by this means that Abelman was encouraged to develop plans to maximise domestic chaos for the Government, and was pointed in the way of Florence Bannister.'

'And Dennistoun has been apprehended as well?' Percy asked.

'He's a floor below us, contemplating a traitor's death,' Kell confirmed. 'Now, since the sponge cake is all gone, I suppose that you'd like to leave?'

'Assuming that we aren't to be shot for what you've revealed to us,' Percy replied.

'No,' Kell said with a smile. 'William will probably grind his teeth when he hears this, but you're too valuable to us, Percy. One day the coach will no doubt arrive to collect you, and we'll expect your total cooperation.'

'Don't hold your breath,' Percy muttered as he rose from his chair and gestured for Jack to leave with him.

It was a cold, drizzly December day, and the Enright family were all huddled around the grave into which Emily Allsop's coffin had just been lowered in the churchyard attached to St Mary's Church, Watford, a short distance from where she'd worked so hard to restore Cassiobury House School. There had been only three distant members of her own family to mourn her passing, so Esther had rounded up everyone she could in order to make the numbers look respectable, and she was sniffling into a handkerchief as Jack held her comfortingly.

'I owe her *so* much,' she said tearfully. 'If it hadn't been for her, I wouldn't even have become an accredited teacher, and as for her last gesture of generosity, I still can't believe it. I only hope I can live up to her ambitions.'

'She had no-one else to leave the school to,' Jack reminded her, 'and everyone I speak to has nothing but praise for Cassiobury House School.'

'Even so,' said Esther, 'I have to be a businesswoman now, as well as a teacher.'

'I'll help all I can,' Annabelle offered as she placed a consoling hand on Esther's other sleeve. 'I owe her a lot, too.

Without her patience with me when I was so unhappy living with my horrid stepfather, I wouldn't have met you and Uncle Jack, and I dread to think where I'd be now. I'd like to become a teacher, like Aunt Esther and that lovely lady we just buried.'

'Percy's stomach is beginning to make noises,' Beattie complained as she drew up alongside them, 'so I hope that Polly put the roast in on time.'

'Time enough to cook it, but not turn it into a funeral pyre,' Percy added from her other side.

'Now that you've completed your investigations into Lucy's theatre, you'll be obliged to stay home more often and eat my "well cooked" offerings, so don't bite the hand that feeds you,' Beattie growled.

'Actually,' Percy fired back, 'I was thinking of taking up acting myself, and perhaps introducing you to the delights of the footlights. If Lucy can be persuaded to make her next Shakespeare classic the one set in Scotland, there's a perfect part for you in the opening act, if you can bring two friends along.'

Annabelle burst out laughing, and Beattie asked, 'What was he getting at, dear?'

'It was a reference to *Macbeth*,' she replied, still giggling. 'It opens with three witches stirring horrible things into a cauldron, and saying things like, "Fillet of a fenny snake, in the caldron boil and bake; eye of newt and toe of frog, wool of bat and tongue of dog." I think he may have been referring to your cooking.'

'Was he indeed?' Beattie replied indignantly, 'Well, see if you can get me that recipe, and that's all he'll eat for a year.'

'That damned Shakespeare has a lot to answer for,' Percy muttered. 'Did he ever write anything with a happy ending?'

A NOTE TO THE READER

Dear Reader,

Thank you for reading this fourth novel in the new Enright series, and I hope that you enjoyed reading it as much as I enjoyed writing it.

As is my usual practice, I began by researching the recorded events of the year in which the main fictitious characters found themselves, and this time they lay in the decade labelled by historians as the Edwardian era. It comes as a surprise to learn that it was a mere ten years in length, given the legacy that it left in the history of England, with its reputation for splendour, ostentatious wealth, lavish social events and more than a hint of decadent scandal.

But it had its darker side, and looming like an approaching storm cloud was the deteriorating relationship between King Edward VII of England and his nephew, Kaiser Wilhelm of Germany, which would eventually explode into The Great War of 1914–1918. At the time in which this novel is set, there was a great deal of underhand intelligence activity being conducted on both sides, as well as an unspoken arms race that led England to develop the *Dreadnought* battleship, with its revolutionary design that enabled it to carry an unprecedented number of heavy-calibre guns, and its new steam turbine propulsion system. The German Navy under Admiral Tirpitz soon began building similar vessels, and given the extent to which both sides in the Anglo-German arms race were spying on each other, it was not stretching the truth too far to develop a plotline in which the *Dreadnought* plans had been leaked to the enemy.

A second plotline was just as valid historically, but more sensitive. Same-sex relationships were illegal during that period, and were to remain so for a further six decades. The risk of prosecution and public shaming had been very publicly underlined by the trial of playwright Oscar Wilde, which is featured in the fifth novel in this series, *The Posing Playwright*. The risk of such consequences opened the door to blackmail, and more than one espionage network, both in that period and later, consisted of men with a secret to keep under wraps for fear of prosecution.

It was also during this same period of English history that it was felt necessary to establish a secret service that could preserve the nation from the consequences of foreign influence for all the wrong reasons. My characters William Melville and Vernon Kell really existed, and carried out the functions described in the pages you have just read. In 1903 Melville had retired as Superintendent of Scotland Yard's Special Branch, in which capacity he had fictionally clashed more than once with Percy Enright (see, for example, my previous novel *The Lost Boys*). He was then immediately recruited to head up a new clandestine Government department known initially as 'MO3' before it morphed, four years later, into the more familiar 'MO5'. He worked under the pseudonym of 'William Morgan' and ran counterintelligence operations against threats to the nation from overseas. He worked alongside Sir Vernon Kell, a former military man and talented multilinguist who took care of clandestine operations abroad, and would become, a few years later, the first Director of the British Security Service, otherwise known as M15, inside which Kell was known only as 'K'.

A few other historical references should be further explained. The local regiment into which Jack and Esther's son seems destined to be drawn was indeed the Hertfordshire Regiment, a reserve force that could be called into active service when required, as they would be in 1914. They did indeed have a drill hall in Watford, and the Earl of Essex was indeed a major in the regiment who was eager to recruit new volunteers.

As for the Women's Social and Political Union, at the time this novel is set they had just embarked on a series of demonstrations in and around Parliament that would lead to the arrest and imprisonment of growing numbers of their members.

The box camera employed by Percy's associate had first been marketed by Eastman Kodak a few years earlier, and had opened the door to amateur photography for tens of thousands of enthusiasts. Instead of a tiresome wait under a tripod-mounted black cloth, and the need to unload heavy glass plates, the photographer simply pressed a button. When the roll of film inside had been used up, they could either develop the images for themselves, or send them to Kodak to do it for them.

Finally, I hope I didn't put too many readers off with my heavy references to Shakespearean drama. The Edwardian era saw a revival of interest in the arts in all their forms, and Shakespeare's plays were a mainstay of many an amateur theatre group. My choice of two of his best-known was clearly in order to provide the murderers with two opportunities for misdeeds with sharp weapons, and reflected my own former interest in amateur dramatics generally, and Shakespearean tragedy in particular. Both *Julius Caesar* and *Hamlet* were school productions in which I appeared many years ago, and — reveal time — I actually played the role of Laertes in *Hamlet*, so was well able to reproduce those parts of it that were relevant to the plot. Apologies if that comes across as self-indulgent, but admit it — you enjoyed the vicarious smell of the greasepaint as well, didn't you?

So what lies ahead for the Enrights? At this stage I have no idea, but hopefully they'll continue to visit me in that transient period between wakefulness and sleep to advise me of what they'd like to get involved with next.

As ever, I would be delighted to see a review of my book posted on **Amazon** or **Goodreads**. Alternatively, feel free to visit, and contact me on, my author website: **davidfieldauthor.com**.

Happy reading!

David

Sapere Books is an exciting new publisher of brilliant fiction and popular history.

To find out more about our latest releases and our monthly bargain books visit our website:
saperebooks.com